Praise for Kassandra Sims and
The Midnight Work

"This is a jaunt into the underworld, where murder is okay if you're hungry, past lives are a given, and fairies wanting to rule the world are to be avoided. And even though she's now part of the undead and rips out the occasional throat, Sophie still wants to buy a Christmas tree and never forgets to take care of her cat. An oddly light-hearted romp mixed in with mayhem, blood, and gore."

—*Romantic Times BookReviews*

"Sims takes risks. . . . The result is a work of imagination and creativity." —*Paperback Reader*

"A fabulous paranormal . . . Kassandra Sims provides a lighthearted-yet-dark humorous tale."

—*Paranormal Romance Reviews*

"Sophie, Suki, and Norah may not be the most lovable of characters ever but they certainly are real. Imagine the cast of *Sex and the City,* only younger, and worried about spilling blood on their designer handbags." —About.com

**Also by Kassandra Sims
from Tor Romance**

The Midnight Work

FALLING

UPWARDS

Kassandra Sims

tor paranormal romance

A TOM DOHERTY ASSOCIATES BOOK
NEW YORK

This is a work of fiction. All the characters and events portrayed in this novel are either fictitious or are used fictitiously.

FALLING UPWARDS

A Tor Book
Published by Tom Doherty Associates, LLC
175 Fifth Avenue
New York, NY 10010

www.tor.com

Tor® is a registered trademark of Tom Doherty Associates, LLC.

ISBN-13: 978-0-765-35581-2
ISBN-10: 0-765-35581-7

First Edition: April 2007

Printed in the United States of America

0 9 8 7 6 5 4 3 2 1

Author's Notes

This entire book was written listening to Jeff Buckley on repeat, especially his live stuff (much of which I suspect is bootleg). There will never be anyone like him. Listen to him while you read this.

To my biscuit, Tina Coker—I love you more than mayonnaise. You endured more than anyone will ever even know of my shenanigans, and you only remind me when you're drunk, so that's special. Oh, don't even start.

To my editor, Anna Genoese—like Cory Branan says, "Nothing scars you more than the things you've never done." I think we understand each other. Thank you for being you.

To my mom and my Aunt Mickey—y'all're the cheese in my grits. The world needs more tenacious Southern women like y'all. Or maybe not, because maybe the world wouldn't survive that.

To all the people who were so beautiful about my first book—I really don't think I would have made it here without you. I appreciate every kind word, every criticism meant to give me a hand up, and every insane piece of commentary. The world turns around people like you. No writer writes in a vacuum. Thank you.

FALLING
UPWARDS

CHAPTER ONE

IN THE EVENING of the third day of her Welsh business trip, Neva Jones found herself in an oddly-named pub, Serpent's Kiss, watching a group of German tourists toss coins into the pub's dominant feature, a large central fountain. Neva had only seen water features like this before in up-market hotels in touristy places like Bangkok, or in chi-chi sushi joints in Manhattan.

She sat in the pub, by a tiny window so encrusted in soot, and grime, and two hundred years of cigarette smoke that she couldn't see out of it. Her table looked old and solid, with the sort of deep brown staining that furniture forgers could never reproduce.

In an effort to take in a little of the local color on her trip, she'd picked this pub on St. Mary's Street at random. Her choice had been based on the level of decay of the façade, the number of Welsh-speakers spilling out of it, and the welcome lack of people under the age of twenty.

The pub scrunched up on itself, a one-room job with a straight bar with brass fixtures set against the wall by the front door. The front door was blessedly devoid of a tinkling bell tolling the arrival of new customers. A television opposite the barkeep, playing soccer, was set high up enough that patrons sitting would have to strain their necks but those standing wouldn't.

She found the fountain oddly attractive. Neva watched the play of light on the surface of the visible water. That was the odd part, even odder than finding a fountain in the middle of a pub in Cardiff—the water rested against the sides of the plain wooden basin (which was something like a barrel with no stays), constantly threatening to spill over the lip—which was carved to look as though a snake rested on it—but never doing so. Quivers and ripples shook the tension of the reflective surface as feet trod over the worn, wooden floorboards around the fountain, but not a drop fell down the sides of the fountain. At odd intervals, a sudden arc of water would shoot from one side of the pool to the other.

Neva was transfixed. The world was a strange and surprising parade of shocks and unlooked-for glories, truly. Neva watched the water, and also observed from the corner of her eye the soap opera at the table next to her, where a young man let down a cavalcade of attractive girls.

She was in Wales with her coworker and superior, James Johnson, and not really enjoying the experience as much as she usually did overseas travel. Even though she was on the team trying to sell the new drug research facility to the city of Cardiff, trying to win tax breaks and land concessions for the sprawling campus, Neva wasn't really sure about Wales. Charming, quirky, full of male voice choirs and coal-mining memorabilia? Sure, Wales had all of that in spades. However, Neva thought Spain would be a cheaper way to break into the E.U. market.

The entire idea behind building a research hub in Europe was to gain inroads into the E.U. by employing hundreds of physicians and pharmacologists and chemists and lower-level, unskilled workers. Youngblood Pharmaceuticals would pump millions of dollars into a wavering economy, winning friends locally and influencing people internationally. Neva had lobbied for Spain because it was more centrally located and alluring for the hotshot talent they wanted to draw to them and away from the competition. Neva just didn't believe Cardiff could hold a candle to Salamanca in that department—cold and rainy versus sunny and brightly colored?

"Now you know, Bethan, I can't possibly come round to Incognito for Slinky night. For one, drum and base is near to the screeching of harpies on a three-day drunk, and for another I've got football to watch." With the sort of soothing, coaxing voice normally used on large dogs and the insane, the young man of about twenty-two at the table next to hers fended off the attentions of a pretty, dark-haired girl with freckles and a pert, up-turned nose. Fourth in a row, that Neva had counted.

"It doesn't have to be that, then, some mates of mine . . ." She spoke with the twisted vowels and strange inflection Neva had been informed originated in The Valleys.

Apparently, "The Valleys" was always said a little meanly, because of hundreds of years of something that Neva read as prejudice. She assumed it was an impoverished, backwards place that other Welsh were ashamed of and didn't want to be associated with. Considering that Neva had been born—and currently lived in—Alabama, she wasn't impressed by this snide prejudice. She'd seen that sort of attitude towards her own self for years in places like California and New York. The impression being, of course, that someone from the South—or, in this case, a smaller town than Cardiff—couldn't be cultured, educated, interesting, or knowledgeable.

Neva polished off her pint of local color and walked the glass back to the bar. The bartender smiled at her with white, even teeth. His eyes were blue and his hair black. That was a theme around Cardiff, she'd noticed. People tended to be darkish, with dark hair. Their eye color varied, but was often brown. Not like when Neva visited Edinburgh a few years back and her dark brown hair, dark brown eyes, and tan skin worked like a corona of neon around her, illuminating her as a foreigner before she even opened her mouth and spoke with an American accent: a southern American accent, but she doubted that made much of a difference.

"Another?" The bartender leaned an elbow against the brass rail on his side of the stained, pocked expanse of wood. Neva couldn't help the reflexive grin at his innate flirtatiousness. This job suited him well, she decided, as he took her glass, fingers brushing hers, winking and tipping his head to the side. "Half-price."

She laughed, shaking her head. "I don't usually drink alone." The words were true, but she regretted them as soon as she said them, because they were an open invitation to any man within the sound of her voice.

The bartender stuck out his hand. "Evan." She shook it, more from well-learned ritual than intent. "Now you're not alone, are you? Besides, you never were, either. That's the entire idea of a pub, publicans, public, not alone."

Neva began to frame a sweet but negative response to Evan, because he really was charming and attractive, but she didn't need to start drinking with a bartender in a city she didn't know in the middle of an important business trip.

"Leave off, Evan, she's an important woman with business to tend." The voice coming from her left shoulder, all sunshine and bright promise, made Neva turn. The voice belonged to the young man from the next table, but now the gentling softness had gone from his tone. He was all wide, wide smile and unblinking eyes.

He stood probably over six foot tall, but Neva tended to judge height by taller-than-her and shorter-than-her. This young man was at least five inches taller than her. The skin on his face curved over sharp cheek bones and a defined jaw line. No creases at his eyes or grooves by the dents on the edges of his smile. She could see why he had to beat the girls off with a stick. Actor or male model material, for sure, with indescribably colored eyes, five colors at once—green, blue, amber, brown, indigo—and gently curling black hair.

Evan-the-bartender looked on at Neva and her new companion with an odd tilt to his head, rubbing a towel back and forth on a spotless section of the bar.

"I don't know about important, but I'm here for work, yeah." Neva pulled out some of the odd-looking coins that apparently masqueraded for money in these parts, and set a few on the bar by the intently curious Evan. His eyes flitted between Neva and the young man, the bar towel hanging limply from his hand.

Evan didn't ask for more money, so Neva waved at him, an odd stillness descending on her and pushing her out into the grey, rain-washed Cardiff evening. She hailed a cab to take her back to her hotel, glancing back towards the door of the Serpent's Kiss. Something unsettling just happened, but she had no idea what. Just *something*.

Unfortunately, she ran into James in the lobby of the

hotel, so her entire plan to waste the rest of the night watching television and puzzling over the oddity of the Serpent's Kiss was blown. The Cardiff research project was James's baby—he was nervous about it, and they were friends, therefore she let him sweep her into the restaurant in the hotel.

Youngblood Pharmaceuticals liked to present itself as the face of the New South. They gave excellent benefit packages, including daycare and same-sex insurance plans. Their hiring policy didn't exactly reflect this twenty-first century ethic, but their public image certainly did. Neva was The Female Executive: she was pretty, she accessorized, she had impeccable credentials as a microbiologist with an MBA. Neva had managed to negotiate a flexible working plan that allowed her to work from home except on those occasions she needed to be trotted out for meetings in California or New York or somewhere in Europe.

James, on the other hand, was The Black Executive. Handsome, articulate, and amusing, he had impeccable credentials as a lawyer with an undergraduate degree in chemistry. He'd managed to convert this resume into being the head of the team responsible for bringing Youngblood onto European soil, and he'd been promised the role of European CEO if the project got the go-ahead.

Neva didn't quite understand James's goals—the spotlight was a glaring place and she was more comfortable in the background, making things work, than in the forefront, leading others. But she and James had similar problems working their ways through the corporate structure, and they contrived to work together a lot because of it, in a binary unit of corporate cooperation that grew from their shared outsider status.

Neva'd kept friends for worse reasons over her thirty-one years.

The restaurant in the hotel played soft jazz, a trumpet and piano piece that she vaguely recognized. Neva shifted her legs under the table, sliding off her ridiculously expensive shoes—an indulgence that still made her feel guilty even though she knew that she made more than enough money to buy a pair a week if she wanted—but some vestiges of her childhood and student years just wouldn't let her go.

The efficient waiter appeared at Neva's elbow. She ordered the fish special. James ordered something with a name that told Neva nothing about what sort of food it was. But she could guess—vegetarian pasta. One of James's quirks was that he never ate meat when he was away from home. He had some complex, nonsensical explanation for that, but Neva knew better than to engage people about the inexplicability of individuality.

"Do some sight-seeing?" James smiled, and Neva returned it. She loved to sight-see. The kitschier, the gaudier, the more absurd or stereotypical, the more she loved it. Her opinion was: bring on the largest ball of twine, the Elvis museum, or, in Cardiff, the Coal Mining Museum.

"No, I didn't really get to do any sight-seeing today. I saw some museum of Welsh culture yesterday. Everyone was speaking Welsh. It was strange." She had actually enjoyed standing in the tide of milling tourists, being stranded in a sea of an incomprehensible language. That particular sort of isolation always made Neva feel more connected to others, because being confused and alone in that way, not able to communicate, was a universal experience. At some point, she figured, everyone would stand in a room and feel like the people around her were speaking a foreign language, even if it was just metaphorical.

James sighed and Neva realized she might have missed him saying something while she mused.

"Sorry, what?" she asked, propping her chin on her fist. She wanted wine. Maybe something crisp and white.

"It's falling apart." James smoothed his red and purple silk tie, fingers running over the sophisticated pattern of concentric circles and dots. He picked up the tumbler full of some kind of whisky Neva couldn't even hope to pronounce. The name fell like melting butter off James's tongue, though. He had a gift for languages. She was sure he'd learn Welsh in no time flat. James really was perfect for this job.

"You know it isn't falling apart, for the love of God." She was herself around him, blue language and taking the Lord's name in vain, opinionated and real. Through being business associates, they'd become friends, even though they only saw each other on business trips like this, since Neva only went to corporate headquarters in Birmingham when something blew up or someone died. She stuck close to her family in south Alabama, stuck close to the coast, to the Gulf, to shrimp and oysters right off the dock, stuck close to her mama and daddy and sisters.

The waiter appeared with their meals, and Neva's mouth watered.

"It looks delicious, thank you," she said to him, as he slid the plate in front of her.

James acknowledged the waiter with a nod, and didn't even pick up his fork. "They want double what we're authorized to give for the land, and they're not budging." He sounded like he was gearing up for some histrionics. They both knew that was the dance, but James needed to work himself up to get the job done. He needed to see the city officials and Welsh assembly members as the enemy, like when he'd played football in college: his team against the other guys, and to the righteous goes the victory.

"You'll fix it all," said Neva, and took a bite of her fish, something local and fresh. Too much lemon in the sauce, not enough capers. She ate it anyway, the beer from the pub had made her starved.

"Okay." James took a deep breath and sat back in the deep dining chair, glass clutched firmly in his hand. "If you didn't go off playing in museums today, what'd you do this afternoon?" Neva could tell he was trying to calm himself down, switch gears, so she indulged him around bites of her fish.

"I checked out the local wildlife. I ended up at some weird bar with this strange fountain thing in it." The side of eggplant was a truly odd combination with the fish, but she ate it all the same.

"Hold up, you went to a bar, in a foreign city, by yourself? You're out your mind." Sometimes James could be old-fashioned and a tad chauvinist. Neva lifted an eyebrow.

"Hello, this is *Wales,* not *Brazil.* And I'm sittin' here, right? Not dead or anything. Get a grip." Neva stared down at her plate, looking away from James, and felt, suddenly, really tired. Tired of meaningless conversation, tired of Wales and wearing pantyhose and the pretty but constricting matching bra and panty set she always felt compelled to wear under her business attire. The classic, black sheath dress that fell just to her knee felt like a shroud. Her hair was pulled uncomfortably tight by its elaborate braiding.

"James . . ."

He met her gaze, and looked concerned, and she felt like a shit. "You getting sick?" he asked. "Foreign food—"

Neva shook her head. "I think I need some sleep. I'm sorry." She pushed away from the table. "Expense this?" Standing, she pulled the napkin off her lap and set it on her plate.

"Hey now, don't get mad at me. I'm just a worrier." He reached up and wrapped a hand around her wrist loosely, looking up with real contrition on his face.

She smiled down at him, forcing it, because he didn't really mean anything by being protective. He saw their ten-year age gap as reason enough to big-brother her sometimes. "Don't sweat it. I'm just having a moment. I'll see you in the mornin'."

Back in her room, Neva slipped out of her dress, hung it up next to all of the other simple but elegant dresses in various shades of black and red—she'd started the affectation early in her career and had become so known for it that she thought the company would grind to a halt if she ever wore blue or green—and sighed as she took off her bra.

The deep, wide, ridiculously extravagant tub beckoned. Neva loved this aspect about traveling for work. Youngblood had to present itself as having endless cashflow and class, so their representatives always stayed in four star hotels with all the perks that entailed.

She poured enough bubble-bath into the water to give her bath a PG rating and slid into the tub. She was asleep in less than five minutes.

Neva dreamt of a wide, still pond reflecting a limitless sky. White clouds drifted across the surface, blowing from one side of the pond to the other. She smelled the crisp tang of apples so strongly she could taste the sour-sweetness on the back of her tongue. Touching the edge of the water, she tried to break the image of the sky with ripples in order to see beneath the surface, but when her fingers sank into the water she fell face first into the pond and just kept falling.

The deflating mass of bubbles clung to her as Neva gasped for air and shot out of the tub. Neva recalled vague images of trees, of lush greenery, of slithering scales, greener still than the plant life, rustling leaves. Standing naked in the pristine hotel bathroom, Neva shook from the cold of waking in tepid bathwater, confused and disoriented.

She dried off, found her safe, yellow cotton pajamas, and laid on top of the covers on the king-sized bed. She turned on the television for white noise, a distraction, and lit on a rugby game with commentary in Welsh.

The slithering, opaque syntax lulled her back into sleep.

The next day's meetings went well without her active participation, which was good, because she was still caught up thinking about her dreams. A man and a snake and an apple, and could her subconscious be any more trite? She wasn't sure what it meant, though, and when she looked down at the notes she was supposed to be taking on Welsh pharmacology law, she had a row of tiny round apples, with perfect leaves on their stems.

"You okay, baby girl?" asked James under his breath as they walked down the hall to lunch.

"Just a little woozy. Not enough caffeine," replied Neva, flashing him her biggest smile and following him into the conference room they were using for lunch.

Her face fell: lunch was a sushi nightmare. Neva loved seafood. But to eat it raw? She never could get used to that—she was a product of south Alabama and the only thing they ate raw there was oysters. She stared at the rows of beautiful but distasteful mounds of rice and seaweed and fish and tried not to gag. She ate a couple of crackers and stayed away from the buffet while James gobbled down the pretty rolls with a huge smile and schmoozed.

A middle-aged burgher in a tatty suit and expensive shoes smiled at her, then plopped down next to her. He stuck out his hand. "How are you finding Cardiff? David Jones."

She smiled. This had already happened to her a couple of times since arriving in Wales. "Neva Jones." She clasped his hand with a firm shake, learned at church at about the age of five, and felt the calluses on his palm. This man had worked for a living. She liked him already for his easy smile and laborer's background.

"Oh, I knew your name, Miss, a person in this room could hardly not. I was just wonderin' if you were Welsh. By extraction, of course." She'd already had this conversation, as well.

"I doubt it, but one can't rule it out, I suppose." Jones was, apparently, just about the most common name in Wales.

"Well you can pretend, or tell me lies, I'll believe whatever you say." David Jones projected the sort of safety and affability that allowed him to say something like that and not set off Neva's warning bells. He was just a natural flirt, like so many of the men she'd met in Cardiff, and judging by his wedding ring and the contentment he projected, he was not trying to pick her up.

"How about if I tell you the truth, which is that I like Cardiff very much, and the people even more, instead?" She smiled and winked, long used to playing along with the softer side of being the female executive. Use what the Lord gave you, her mama said. Neva had resisted using that type of flirtatious manipulation for the first several years in the business world. She gave up when she realized that her one-woman crusade would be better applied to the glass ceiling rather than to shuffling papers, and what sort of business attire she wore.

Neva let David Jones steer her into conversation with five other men of similar age, all of them pleasant and affable. They reminded her of southerners, really, and gave her a queer longing in the pit of her stomach for the home she'd only left a few days ago.

After a productive afternoon, Neva begged off supper with James and went back to her room. She changed out of her work clothes and into comfortable boots, jeans, and a soft cashmere-lambswool handmade sweater over an old Duke University t-shirt. Both tops were light blue, and the sweater was made by her mama, who knit up a storm even though no one could hardly ever wear her handiwork since was it only sweater weather in south Alabama about three weeks out of the year.

Neva set off from the hotel, planning to stop in at a small bistro and have a sandwich and salad. Instead, she found herself ambling through the chilly spitting rain until she stood outside the Serpent's Kiss, again staring at the smudged windows and bright red front door.

Apple red.

Funny how she hadn't noticed that before.

"Coming inside?"

Neva's mind burst with thoughts of brilliant, blinding sunshine and hope. She turned to see the man from the night before looking at her with raised eyebrows and a twisted grin. He slouched on the sidewalk in loose-fitting jeans, battered Adidas, and an ancient brown corduroy jacket.

"Do they have food?" As she asked it, her body remembered it wanted supper and she felt suddenly light-headed.

"The best fish and chips in Cardiff Town; come on, then, you're on the verge of collapse." He reached out a hand towards her elbow, but Neva pulled away before he could touch her. James was right about being careful. A young, pretty face and toned body didn't make this kid safe, and she sure as hell wasn't going to put herself into a position where he could use his size against her.

"Okay, good." She turned and flung open the door to the pub. There were enough people inside that even if the kid *was* a threat, he couldn't do much besides look pretty at her.

"Hey there!" Evan waved his towel at her from across the bar. Neva smiled back at him. The water in the fountain jumped as she wound around it.

"What'll it be?" Slapping his hand on the top of the bar, Evan pointed with his other hand towards the taps.

"Actually, could I get an order of fish and chips?" She pulled one of the bar stools out with her foot and climbed up on it.

"Ah, sure thing." Evan winked. "What sort of fish?"

Neva hadn't been aware there was more than one variety of fish in fish and chips.

"There's more than one kind?" She blinked rapidly in the universal sign of confusion. She'd assumed there were schools of chip-fish swimming around in the North Atlantic just waiting to be scooped into little, round-bottomed boats and hauled away to be battered up and fried golden brown.

"Haddock, cod, plaice, whiting . . ." Evan ticked the types of fish off on his fingers.

None of those fish rang any taste bells for Neva. Her knowledge of fish ran to the Gulf of Mexico species, like snapper and amberjack.

"Just give her cod and have done with your silliness." The guy in the corduroy jacket plunked himself down on the stool next to hers, and Neva gave him the hairy eyeball.

"Is that the good kind?" What was his deal, anyway? Even right then some nubile young thing was sidling up to him, smiling, reaching out for his arm. He turned to the girl, not getting a chance to answer Neva.

"Cod it is." Evan ambled off through a door beyond the rows and rows of bottles of alcohol.

Neva watched the rugby match on the television on the wall at the back of the bar and pretended not to listen to the kid and his newest admirer.

"You look fit tonight, March," the girl said. Her accent was different from the local one, less burnished somehow.

"Thanks, Katie. New shoes?" March (and that was a really strange name, Neva decided instantly) rejoined with obvious boredom.

"Not really, they're Claire's," Katie sighed. Neva had no idea what the hell was going on with these people. She felt like she'd walked onto the set of a soap opera and hadn't been handed a script.

"Wanna pint, then, to tide you over until your proper food comes?" Evan's voice pulled Neva out of her idyll.

She swung back around and saw a piece of bread slathered with butter sitting on a chipped brown plate. Evan smiled. "You looked peckish. Go on, then."

Neva thanked him with a beaming smile, picked up the brown bread and took a huge bite. It was sweet and nutty, homemade bread nirvana. Before she could refuse the pint, Evan was pulling it, dark amber liquid flowing into the glass.

She chewed and swallowed, and chased the bread with a huge gulp of beer when it was set in front of her. She felt oddly content with her bread and butter and beer in this dingy, smoky, off-kilter place.

"Katie, what do you want me to say?" March sounded pinched, annoyed, on the edge of anger. Neva tuned back into the conversation next to her, eating her bread and openly staring at the arguing pair.

"I want you to say 'yes, Katie, I'll go with you to dinner', or something like that, then." Neva scoped out

Katie. She was roundish, with huge boobs and curvy hips; she sported thick red hair and a navy blue pea coat. She was also extremely angry.

"Look, Katie, I'd love to say something like that, but I'm not available, like I've said . . ."

Katie cut him off. "Oh, that. I've heard it time and again, where's this girlfriend no one's ever met, huh?"

And Neva felt something strange shift inside her, like her whole body was flipped upside down and then set right again so fast it was almost imperceptible. The flash of vertigo passed, and Neva felt the spray off the leaping water in the fountain.

"March, introduce me to your friend." The words slid out of Neva's mouth almost like she was a puppet; Neva heard them, but she couldn't remember thinking them. She felt like she was under water, moving against its pressure.

Katie's mouth fell open like someone had slapped her with an invisible hand. On the very edge of her peripheral vision, Neva caught Evan dropping a bottle on the ground with a loud, reverberating thud.

But March's reaction was something else entirely. He turned slowly, and in the strange atmosphere it looked almost like stop-motion animation.

"There's that, then," he said, but not in English. His mouth drifted over too many slippery vowels and undulating dental consonants for that. Neva understood him all the same. She understood that he was acknowledging her in a way that no one ever had before, totally and to the bone, with no judgment and no hesitation.

"Katie, this is Neva Jones." He wasn't looking at Katie, though; his eyes never left Neva's face, his expression was almost resigned.

"A Yank? Why'd you never mention before your girl

was American?" Katie's voice strained toward a register at least two higher than normal, but Neva barely heard her at all.

March braced a hand against the bar, blocking Katie from Neva's sight. His pupils dilated in the darkness of the bar leaving only a rim of grey-blue wedged between black and white. "When you were a very young girl, before you began school or wore shoes reflexively, did you ever dream of music as notes of colors, alive and . . ."

"Falling upwards through the sky into a bowl of standing water where the sun should have been." Neva finished.

The smile that curved on March's face wasn't young, and it wasn't careful and happy. He smiled with black humor, with knowledge no one twenty-two should have.

"Ah, lass. You lot get younger and younger all the while thinking yourselves so world-weary. You don't heed the spark inside, the echo of truth that tells you something odd is happening, something unlooked for." He reached a finger out and touched the scar on the underside of Neva's chin. She'd gotten it as a child, clipping her face on the edge of the sidewalk trying to roller skate. "You're very innocent. It smells like grass broken underfoot and fresh water." His hand dropped, and he looked tired.

"Well, at least you like to travel," he said, throwing his head back and laughing deeply, setting the hair on the backs of Neva's arms on end.

She looked away, and the *flip-flop-whoosh* of vertigo hit her again. Reaching her hand out to steady herself, she met skin and hard, sharp bones beneath. When the threat of falling to the floor passed, she looked up to see her hand clutched in March's. He held up a thick, homemade French fry.

"The chips here are brilliant." He popped the fry in his mouth and chewed, smiling. His smile probably had women dropping their panties in a fifty foot radius.

Neva considered freaking out. Then she chalked her displaced, dislocated feelings up to low blood sugar and jetlag. She turned to her plate and picked up a piece of fish, not even bothering to use a fork.

She chewed, looking up to thank Evan. His back was to her as he diligently polished glasses.

"Don't be offended when he goes cold on you. It's nothing personal." Neva cut March a hard look. His smile had slid off, and he watched her with curiosity written plain on his perfectly formed face.

"What d'you mean? He's a natural born flirt."

March reached out and grabbed a bottle of vinegar off the bar, spritzing all the food on the plate with the light brown, noxious substance, thereby ruining Neva's entire meal.

"What the hell are you doing?" She stared in horror at the wreck of her lovely meal of deep-fried happiness.

His forehead creased and his eyebrows came down into a V. "Fixing up the fish and chips."

"No, you just doused my supper with vinegar, which I loathe. Evan!" She was on the verge of smacking March up-side the head.

Evan turned around, face placid, reserved. He strode over with clipped movements, towel and glass still in hand. "Yes, Miss, how can I be of service?"

Neva just stared at him. Had he been body-snatched right under her nose? Was this some kind of joke on her? Either she was suffering from severe culture shock, combined with jetlag—or something really strange was going on here.

"Evan?" She tried again.

He stood, straight-back and lock-kneed, no smile, no winks, no saucy leaning on the bar. "Yes, Miss?"

"I told you not to take it personally." March sighed next to her.

The fumes of vinegar, beer, and fried food suddenly smothered her, and Neva jumped down off her stool. She rummaged in her pocket for a few five pound notes. She didn't bother to ask what she owed, just tossed some money on the counter and high-tailed it out of the Twilight Zone.

The rain had picked up while she was inside and a gust of wind blew the drops sideways at her. From the stinging on her face, she thought the rain was degenerating into sleet. She walked a few minutes in a bubble of confusion and fright before she hailed a cab.

She fell asleep in the taxi on the way back to the hotel and woke with the terrified cabbie shaking her and demanding she not be dead. She obliged him. The walk through the lobby took as much effort as walking through knee-deep water. The journey up to her room felt like blessed respite, and Neva had to fight to stay awake even the scant seconds the ascent to her floor took. She was still hungry, but too exhausted to bother ordering.

She collapsed face-first on the duvet, still dressed in her wet clothes, and slept like the dead.

Neva heard a far-away banging sound and struggled to pull herself up off the ocean floor. She couldn't breathe, couldn't move. The scream remained still-born in her unyielding mouth.

Finally, she snapped her lips open and yanked a lungful of air, gasping. Her heart beat in her ears and her pulse leaped, trying to escape the barrier of her skin. Scrabbling out of bed, she ran to the door and flung it open.

James stood on the other side, fully dressed. His expression shifted from annoyed to worried when he looked at her. "Neva, baby, are you all right?" He reached out and grabbed her elbow.

She was not all right, but she had no idea what was wrong. Everything? She had no name for what she felt. Unhinged, frightened, distant.

"What's up? I guess I over-slept." Neva pulled her elbow out of James' hand and stepped back into her room. He followed, eyeing her.

"Fine, don't tell me whatever deep, dark, perverted secret you got. I'd rather not know, so I can go for plausible deniability when you're arrested by Interpol." He had started off light, matching his words, but by the end of his little speech, James's voice had dropped to serious, intent. She knew he wouldn't press, though.

"Sorry, I'll get dressed and come downstairs." She really wanted to get him out of there so she could be weirded-out in peace.

"No point. Meetings are cancelled. You won't believe this: David Jones had a massive coronary last night, and the whole issue's pushed back until they shuffle around the responsibility he can't shoulder from his hospital bed." James was obviously crushed. She wanted to comfort him, tell him all the right things about it being a temporary setback, and how the deal was totally green-light all the way, but she couldn't force the words out of her mouth. There seemed to be an invisible wall of water between them, and Neva felt like the effort to breach it was just far too much. She felt even more horrible that she didn't feel worse for David Jones—he'd seemed like a genuinely nice guy who deserved a far better fate. She felt for him and his family both.

"I'll call and reschedule our tickets. We can leave at six-thirty tomorrow morning." He paused when she didn't say anything. "Are you okay? Really."

She wasn't okay. She wasn't sure what she was, but it wasn't okay. "Yeah, I'm great. Don't worry about my ticket. I'll take a couple of vacation days, stay here until the original departure date." She had no idea why she said that. Did she want to stay here? Maybe this was entropy, easier to just remain in the path she was already walking.

"Yeah, okay." He eyed her, opened his mouth to say something else, but thought better of it. "Go back to bed. I'll show myself out."

She did, and he did.

Neva woke up again, and the open drapes in the bedroom only let in shadows from streetlights. She sat up, her jeans rubbing her, her sweater itchy against her neck, and she almost laughed. In her lethargy she felt safe, the familiar feeling of doing something useless and reckless like sleeping through business meetings and waking up at—she looked at the clock by the bed—after nine p.m. reminded her of college, of the person she was before she traded cut-offs and holey shirts for sensible business attire and a briefcase.

She rolled out of bed, pulling her sweater and shirt off, amazed that in the walking coma of the night before she'd remembered and managed to get her bra off. Her agenda was as follows: shower, clean clothes, coffee.

After she stood in the shower under the hot water until her skin pruned, she dug around in her suitcase and extracted a pair of thin-wale corduroys with the sort of low-rise waistband that fell below her bellybutton but didn't make her reach down and pull her pants up constantly, fearing they were about to hit her ankles. She wore comfortable, ratty underwear and a bra so spizzle-sprung it was hardly even effective for its intended purpose. A Violent Femmes t-shirt from circa 1994 and another one of her mama's homemade sweaters—this one black and white and red with capering reindeer along the front—completed her outfit, and she was out the door.

The lobby swarmed with French business people and Neva threaded through the crowd to the restaurant, buoyed by Armani and the smell of tobacco on fabric.

Parking herself in an alcove, hidden by a half wall and a profusion of potted trees bedecked with tiny white lights, she motioned energetically to the waiter. He approached with the sort of lazy charm, a half smile on his face and a loose spring in his step, that she'd come to expect in Cardiff. "What would Miss like this evening?" And there were about fifty invitations embedded there.

"Coffee." She didn't smile at him, so that he wouldn't be encouraged to wink or write his number on the back of her bill. She'd never had so much male attention in her life. Neva was starting to think perhaps there was something in the local water supply.

"You'll be awake all night." And the wink made its gallant appearance. She rolled her eyes, and the waiter laughed, not put off in the least. He did stroll off all the same.

"The hell is wrong with the men here?" she mumbled to herself, and wished she'd brought a book down with her or picked up one of the myriad newspapers by the hostess's stand.

"It's not them, it's you. They can hear the echo of your music in their souls." March's voice intruded on Neva's internal grousing. Her head snapped up, and she watched him pull out a chair and park himself brazenly at her table, scooting his chair closer.

Neva had many flaws—an addiction to cholesterol-laden foodstuffs, a disinclination to use sunscreen, a desire to sit too close to the television ("You'll burn your brain out with radiation!" her grandma warned), a fondness for alcohol, a tendency to cut off other people as they spoke and dismiss their opinions as ridiculous—but no one could ever accuse her of being self-delusional. She was damned hard on herself most of the time. She could admit freely that this guy was freaking hot. But he was also probably ten years younger than her thirty-one. He might not have even cleared his second decade yet, and while her sister often critiqued teenaged boys in school uniforms with the excuse of "Hey, it's their fantasy, you know. Go on, ask one out, see what happens," Neva had serious issues with that kind of jettisoning of social mores. Sure, a nineteen-year-old might be fine, and enthusiastic in bed, but what would you talk to him about? His homework?

Not that March had made any overtures towards her, really. All he'd done was act like a freak, turn down dates, and ruin her supper.

"Did you follow me here?"

The waiter showed up with her coffee, cutting a wide swath around March. Neva watched March watch the other man, the way the waiter didn't let his eyes touch March's face. Yeah, something really strange centered around March, and Neva wasn't thrilled with it at all. The waiter practically sprinted away as soon as the carafe of coffee touched the table.

"No." March leaned forward, bracing his arms on the tabletop and leaning within a foot of Neva. "Can you ride a horse?"

Neva didn't move away from him, didn't concede in any way that he was weirding her out. She blinked slowly and sipped her coffee. He had to be lying about following her, but aside from the usual reasons—being a psychopathic killer or a very poor stalker—she had no idea why he'd follow her only to ask her strange questions and scare the waiters with his pheromones or whatever.

"My daddy's people own horse farms. I've ridden all my life." The coffee tasted bitter.

March sighed. He smelled like tart apples and sun-baked denim. "What kind of horses?" His voice broke around the 'or' in horses, like he'd smoked too many cigarettes the night before, the tobacco giving his voice a dark sheen, low and swirling like spoken whisky.

"Quarter horses." Why she even entertained this conversation, Neva couldn't have said. She felt like she was being pulled back and forth in a strong riptide. She could fight it, but that would only drown her faster.

"Can you hunt?" He was closer, but she didn't see him move. His hand reached up and gently lifted the coffee cup from her fingers, and she yielded it without demur.

"I've never killed anything but a possum, but I know how to, yeah." She came from sturdy, reliable, redneck stock. She could hunt and fish and even shoot a bow with some accuracy.

"Fewer and fewer people can, these days." March smiled, but all Neva saw there was weary sadness, some kind of lingering pain. "Fewer and fewer, and one day there will be none. What will happen then, when none can hunt and none can ride, when the leaves in the forests are silent and the beasts flee not from a bow but from the encroachment of machines and wholesale destruction?" As he spoke, Neva saw a still glade in her mind; in the midst of the glade was a pond that reflected the sky, the convex bowl of the sky flattened and elongated, white clouds drifting across the glassy water.

"May every spirit forbid such." The words tumbled from her lips bent back and scrambled into another language, but it felt natural—totally natural—that they should.

March's sad smile flipped up, and he laughed, tossing his head back. "Oh, what more killing emotion is there to the doomed than hope, lass? None. But there hasn't been one like you for far too long."

* * *

Neva woke up suddenly in her hotel room, shadows cavorting on the ceiling from strobing car headlights and streetlights. The clock by her bed read 10:15. She picked up the phone and had the concierge connect her to British Airways. She changed her flight to accompany James back to Alabama.

CHAPTER TWO

SPRING IN MOBILE was less of a slow slide into warmth and sprouting bulbs and more of a sudden onslaught of humidity and a devolution into perpetual rain. The clouds rolled in off the Gulf in succeeding waves, breaking and flooding south Alabama in a way that, apparently, the city planners hadn't been expecting, even though the micro-climate was ancient.

Irritatingly pronounced every which way by foreigners: Mob-Isle, MO-bile or anything rather than the normal, Mo-Beel sat high in the northwestern corner of a long, deep bay (named, appropriately enough, Mobile Bay) that was really an inlet of the Gulf of Mexico. Mobile, surprisingly, was the second largest metropolitan area in Alabama. People wanted to live there despite cockroaches the size of small dogs, the sixty-four inch annual rainfall (the heaviest in the U.S.) and even despite the weird Do-Da parade in which the residents dressed up their dogs in fancy dress and walked down the street as though this was something to be proud of.

Most people lived out in the county in the stretch of strip malls, airport, and concrete called West Mobile. A few people, longing for the ephemeral, mythical Southern small town life, had moved across Mobile Bay into Baldwin county, with its once-charming but now affected shore communities.

Neva Jones lived in Mobile proper, in the gentrified, Craftsman home stretch that buffeted the reclaimed, bar-laden downtown from the poorer neighborhoods and government housing.

Semmes Avenue sprawled in cracked concrete-streeted glory. Each house was a tiny reflection of its owner's personality. Neva had unwittingly moved into a gay enclave when she purchased her home. Both of her neighbors on either side were gay men. The neighbor across the street was a lesbian. At first she was worried they would reject her, freeze her out of the street parties and calendar of barbeques. Instead, she'd become the neighborhood pet of a sort, the straight girl who always needed her hair done, a broken toilet mended, or a manicure. She filled in on the neighborhood softball team. She was also always in danger of being fixed up with someone's "adorable" brother.

She got used to it—and came to almost enjoy it—very quickly.

Her house was a neat pale yellow Craftsman with a wide deep porch suspended by the sort of thin at the top, thick at the bottom columns that Craftsmen homes were famous for. Her roof sported a triangular cupola, the adornment giving the impression of a second story, but that really functioned as a skylight in her foyer. Her floors stretched out in unbroken heart-of-pine, restored by herself, her sister, several neighbors, and her daddy—who mainly told stories about fishing and cooked supper on the grill since his knees were too bad to get down low like that. Each room had its own personality, its own color.

The foyer copied the exterior in yellow, but a brighter, more lemony shade that twisted back over and under the six-inch white moldings and into to the kitchen. The kitchen stretched across the back of the house from the exterior wall to the pantry, which had been converted to a laundry room. The walls were a 1950s-era teal, the counters black and white tile, the floors set in larger black and white tile.

Through the pantry stood a bedroom, the back-most of three interconnected bedrooms that piled on top of one another in the traditional shotgun pattern. Shotgun houses were built so that the front room lead directly to the next room, with no hallways or connective areas. Room to room to room. The name came from the old saying that in such houses, a person could shoot a gun from the front door, and hit someone on the back porch. The first of these rooms in Neva's house was accessible from an archway in the foyer; it had been converted into Neva's office. The middle one was used, in theory, as a guest room, and connected to the bathroom. On the left side of the house was a formal living room, long since devolved into a rec room with a television and all the accoutrements of settled, middle class life. Neva could see straight from her front porch into the kitchen at the back of the house, if all the connecting doors were left open— which they usually were.

The house constantly looked as though a gang of teenagers had ransacked it. Neva had thanked God when her mother moved across the Bay to Fairhope, because that meant she wouldn't drop by at every waking hour and spout a running commentary about Neva's abysmal housekeeping abilities. She had a cleaning lady who came by once a month. Sometimes her neighbor, Jay, would saunter through her rarely locked back door and unload the dishwasher for her or clean out her refrigerator. He enjoyed feeling superior, and Neva enjoyed not doing the work herself.

One job she never skimped on was cleaning the litter box, however. Neva had three cats—Pyewacket, a long-haired, solid black behemoth; Bruce, a long-haired ginger descended from the original mouser on her grandparents' farm; and Lex, a Russian Blue pedigree that she got from one of her neighbors who ran an at-home animal rescue operation. Not one of the cats was under 20 pounds, but Pyewacket took the prize at 26.

Because she worked from home, some days, the only people Neva talked to were her cats. She would have got out her BB gun if someone tried to tell her they weren't people. Working from home could be like that, solitary and quiet. She had her routine: up at eight, coffee, work solid to noon, eat, shower, work another couple of hours, the evening news, *Dr. Who* reruns if she could find some and whatever was on PBS if she couldn't. Her neighbors saw her as something of a hard-luck case, so they would stop by bearing casseroles or invitations to church or to meet their brothers. She was polite. They were her friends and meant well, but Neva just hadn't been the same since she'd returned from Wales a few weeks before.

She'd started to think some of her daddy's family's mental illness might have found her. The oddest occurrences happened to her since coming back, and she couldn't shake them. After a while, she told her mama and sister. They laughed her off. Until Mardi Gras.

People associate Mardi Gras with New Orleans, with bared breasts and bacchanals in the streets. But Mardi Gras was just the Gulf Coast Creole name for Carnival. The French colonialists brought their language, their religion, and their holidays with them when they settled the Gulf Coast from North Florida to Louisiana. Neva's parents were in The Order of the Incas Mardi Gras society—one of the many groups that put on parades and formal balls culminating on Mardi Gras Day, Fat Tuesday, the day before the beginning of Lent in the Catholic calendar.

From the time she was small, Neva had helped with the floats, making papier-maché flowers or animals or sea creatures, depending on the city-wide Mardi Gras theme of the year. That year, in the Mardi Gras after Neva went on business in Wales and had a very strange experience indeed, the theme was Good and Evil. The Order of the Incas committee decided their float would be dominated by a giant apple tree, and the float-riders would wear various snake-motif ensembles. Neva was enlisted to help with the tree.

"It's not like you have to go to work," her mama said. That was what people always said when Neva told them she worked from home. She didn't bother to argue about that anymore.

Neva made molds out of chicken wire and began constructing hundreds of papier-maché apples. She would wake up in the morning, go down to her kitchen, and fold chicken wire into an applish sort of shape, pour water and Elmer's glue into a bowl, and rip up pieces of paper. Scrap of paper over scrap of paper, she shaped paper apples. It became almost a meditative experience; she lost track of the movements of her fingers, of the feel of the vinyl and metal chair beneath her, and she chased some elusive chime in her mind. She drifted away from life and into a world where nothing existed but apples, the odd whinny of a horse, and music drifting through the air like million-faceted crystals.

Sometimes, she didn't need the paper apples to get to that place. She'd be in the middle of a business call, listening to her assistant in Birmingham rattling off figures and projections for revenue streams and somewhere far off she'd hear the chimes like the half-remembered chimes in the Serpent's Kiss. The next thing she'd know, her assistant Heather would be saying "Hello, hello, Neva? Are you there? Are you all right? I can hear you breathing!"

So as Mardi Gras drew nearer and nearer Neva made more and more apples and let herself slip down into her still place of water and music. This came to a halt when Nadia, her sister, showed up unexpectedly, stomping around the kitchen, having a total melt-down.

"Seriously, I'm worried about you!" The words snapped Neva back from gazing into a still pond reflecting a vast, moving sky.

"What? What the hell are you doing here?" Neva thought the best way to deal with her sister was anger. Okay so perhaps she didn't *think* so much as just react.

Lex slithered through the kitty door, imperious blue eyes turned on Nadia. Neva really wished he was some kind of attack cat and could do more than just stare someone into submission.

"Okay, I stand here for ten minutes screaming, and that's all you have to say? For real, Neva, I think you have epilepsy. The flashing lights in your peripheral vision—"

"They aren't flashing lights! They're something reflective." Neva cut in and really wished she hadn't.

"Uh huh. The music thing? That's another symptom. Hearing music." Nadia put her hands on her hips and glared. Neva wasn't impressed. They looked too much alike, had the same facial expressions, for Neva to be intimidated. Nadia was a lawyer and thought that her rhetoric should reduce anyone to a heap of quivering compliance.

"You're making that up." Naturally, Neva had considered that she had epilepsy. She'd done some research. Mostly her symptoms tilted a lot harder towards psychosis than epilepsy.

"So what if I am? You still need to get checked out." Her voice going shrill, Nadia paced the kitchen back and forth, her heels clicking on the tiles. She wore a black pantsuit with a white silk blouse. They had the color scheme habit in common, along with their mother's dark looks and her inclination to be persnickety enough to be borderline obsessive compulsive. Nadia applied her OCD to all aspects of her life, from the detailing on her car to the way her shoes were always perfectly aligned in her closet to the fact that she only ever dated blonds. Neva had a milder case, and only got worked up over things on her desk being moved or having to check that the coffee pot was turned off five times in a row.

Since Nadia's newest blond boy was a shrink, Neva was suspicious. "Is this some kind of intervention where you invite me to supper then drive me to the loonybin?"

Her sister's face went tight enough that Neva realized she really had intended to do that. "You're shitting me. Get out of here. Don't come back until you get a grip." Neva turned back to her apples, not really all that mad. She'd expected something like that from Nadia. She was so straight-laced, so regimented. She even thought yellow cars were gauche.

"I'm only trying to help you." Nadia tried for genuine, almost achieving it, but Neva just didn't buy it.

"No, you're just trying to make sure your nutbar sister gets medicated before you try to make partner. Don't make me call Donnie." Donnie was their cousin, a sheriff's deputy.

"You wouldn't even." Nadia spat out, the click-clack of her heels stilling.

"I surely would! I'd get a restraining order, too. How'd that look? Get out!" Neva leaped out of her chair, sending it skittering back and Lex meowing like crazy, running in a circle of confusion. Nadia just glared.

"This isn't 1943, being crazy isn't endearingly Southern and charming. I can get you put up someplace *non compos mentis,* and if you go off doin' something in public, don't think I won't!" She turned, her sensible bob swinging around her perfectly done-up face and flounced out the back door.

Immediately, Neva picked up the phone and called her mama.

"Yello'!" Since she'd retired, all her mama did was garden, go to art galleries with her own sister, Ida, who lived up the street from her, and go to every single outdoor festival within a day's drive.

"Mama, do you think I'm goin' crazy?" The chirping of birds sounded down the line. Her mama was out in the garden.

"Nadia drop by?" She was amused. Neva plunked back down at the table with her apples.

"So how long's she been tryin' to get me locked up?" The anger made her feel righteous, like there was no doubt on God's green earth that Nadia was Satan incarnate and trying to screw up Neva's entire life. They'd always fought like cats and dogs.

"She didn't say that, did she?" The amused tone calmed

Neva down slightly. They really did have some head cases on her daddy's side, and so Neva knew that if her mama said no, her sister couldn't lock Neva up. One nay-saying family member could send the whole matter to court if the subject of the interment wasn't a direct threat to herself or someone else. Neva hadn't hurt herself or anyone else.

"Yeah, she totally did. She's an evil changeling." Bruce jumped up on the table and started batting the apples off onto the floor. Neva didn't bother to stop him, since he'd just keeping knocking them all off over and over again if she picked them up.

"Aw, mama's baby, you know your sister doesn't mean anything by it, she's just so focused, driven . . ."

"A bitch." Neva cut in.

Her mother cracked up, laughing loud and freely. "Yeah, well, who can't be? How's them apples comin'?"

"Got about twenty finished and ready to be painted. You think I should do 'em all red, or what?"

The rest of the call was pretty much all about Mardi Gras, her Meemaw's fig preserves, and who was going to bake the King Cakes that year.

On the Thursday of the week before Mardi Gras, Neva thought she saw something impossible in her bathroom mirror. She'd taken a hot shower, and the whole room was steamed up pretty fierce. She toweled her hair dry, rubbing vigorously. As she dropped the towel from her head, the condensation on the mirror suddenly evaporated, leaving the image of a riotous wood overgrown with brambles and vines with small, mammalian creatures leaping from branch to branch. Behind her, she heard the high, clear sound of a glass chiming, and she whirled around. There was nothing there, and when she turned back to look at the mirror it was just a clouded bathroom mirror. She reached out and wiped her hand against the glass, and when the water streaked under her palm exposed a cleared space, all she saw was her own face staring back.

Oddly, she wasn't scared. Since her sister had confronted her with the option of insanity, Neva had sort of accepted it. If she was nuts, she'd be nuts and not scared of her own mind. Unless it told her to stand in traffic or stab someone. Until then, she'd face down her hallucinations be they visual or auditory.

She worked the rest of the day, clean through supper, and she even missed the first ten minutes of the news.

That night she went to a cookout at Jay's. She ate oysters fresh off the boat with Tabasco and horseradish on saltines and fended off several attempts to fix her up with available brothers. She drank four Coronas to chase the bite of the horseradish, overdid it a little, and fell asleep by nine thirty.

Neva dreamt of an impossible orchard of red and gold variegated apples. The trees climbed so high they blocked all but the most persistent rays of sunshine. The canopy swayed in breezes Neva couldn't feel. She knew somewhere beyond the forever-long stretch of trees the high, perfect music played. Picking up her foot, she tried to walk towards the music, to find it, to hear it, just once all strung together.

"You're very hard to reach." Turning her head took heroic effort, as though her body were caught in drying cement she couldn't see. From the corner of her eye, standing behind her to the left, was March, the boy from Cardiff.

She couldn't speak no matter how hard she tried.

"You live so near to water, it shouldn't be so difficult. Do you love your life so very much?" He paused and took one step further into her line of sight. She could see he wore high leather boots and a tunic of some kind. He held a fishing net in his left hand.

"It grows harder and harder each time to touch someone's dreams. You flow further and further from here. Soon you will be only myths to us, stories told and disbelieved. Can you imagine?" March smiled, but she saw nothing by sorrow there; he laughed all the same, manic and frightening.

"If you will not come to me, then you cannot even fail. Maybe that's better than me finding hope again only to be devastated?" He paused again, tilting his head to the side. "But you did surprise me, Neva Jones, and for three seconds in time, an infinity and a heartbeat, I felt that hope again. Will you not even try to help me?"

Neva's dream drifted away from the beautiful boy in his apple orchard. She slipped into a dream of a courtroom in which her mother's garden was on trial for color scheme infractions.

The next morning, Neva made a couple of decisions. The first was that she was going to take off from work for the week before Mardi Grass Week as well as Mardi Gras Week. She had about a year's worth of vacation days, no pressing projects, and Youngblood Pharmaceuticals believed in "flex-time". She made a couple calls, sent off a fax with her signature, and shut her computer off for two weeks. Not really, she knew someone would call her in a panic, and she'd get done what needed getting done, but it was fun pretending while it lasted.

The second important decision she made was to call her neighbor, Jay's boyfriend, Tony, to go shopping with her for dresses for the round of Balls that would soon commence. Mardi Gras Balls were proms for adults. Everyone got dressed to the hilt, got drunk and laid, and puked in their best friend's car. But instead of just one night, the festivities lasted for a month. Up to now, Neva had refused tickets for various parties and Balls. She'd been trying to decide if she was on the verge of a nervous breakdown or hospitalization.

Instead, she embraced her eccentric imaginings and strange dreams—because who wouldn't dream about a boy like March?—and jumped off the deep end of the pier into shopping for formal-wear with a drag queen.

"Hey," Neva said when Tony answered the phone. Miss Antoinetta, when not rocking the spangles and platforms, was a well-respected English professor at the University of South Alabama. He didn't have tenure, therefore no one mentioned his hobby when in a mixed crowd. Neva loved him to bits and pieces.

"Hey, honey," Tony was obviously in his car, Pet Shop Boys blaring out of the speakers.

"So, I was thinkin' . . ."

"That you'd give up being a hermit and get out there where the boys are? Uh huh." He turned down the radio, obviously in stop-and-go traffic on Airport Boulevard coming back from West Mobile and the University's campus.

"Did you hear I'm goin' crazy? Cut a crazy girl a break." She laughed at herself, because what else could she do?

"Honey, if I only got laid once a year, I'd be crazy, too. You're just repressed. Ima fix you up." Tony sounded way too enthused. She knew that was a bad sign, but screw it.

"A'ight, as long as I get fake eyelashes, we're cool like the other side of the pillow."

"Be there after I change."

"Over and out, scout." Neva hung the phone up and walked to the bathroom to hop in the shower, her second of the day with the heat already seeping in and making her sweat like a hog, even though it was just the last week of February. Some years were hotter than others, and that winter had only lasted three weeks in January.

She showered. Toweling her hair off, she bravely looked into the foggy mirror, but all she saw was grey condensation. Because she'd have to pull her clothes on and off ad infinitum, she chose a simple old A-line dress with short sleeves to wear and slipped into a pair of Birkenstocks.

"Oh girl, no!" Tony didn't bother to knock. He strode into the kitchen carrying Bruce in his arms, the ginger cat trying to lick Tony's face while Tony kept his neck strained to the side to prevent it. "You are not really wearin' that."

The dress *was* rather sack-like, but one could never live up to the fashion standards of a drag queen. She didn't even try.

Tony stood 6' 1" in bare feet and a staggering 6' 6" in his heels. His buffed, moisturized skin glowed café-au-lait and matched his grey eyes and toned body. He was dreamy, a little fey, and could be catty from time to time. He specialized in Southern lit and could quote Eudora Welty or Zora Neale Hurston with equal vigor, collected art glass, and drove the same car he'd bought at seventeen—a 1981 Toyota Corolla, beige.

"This is what I'm wearing." Neva grabbed her car keys, because Lord knew she wasn't riding in Tony's deathtrap with no air conditioning, and headed to the back door.

He set the cat down and followed, ambling, opening drawers and cabinets as he went. "Where y'all hide y'all's paper bags, because I'm not gon' be seen in public with no one wearing that get up."

She ignored him and opened the door to her forest green Volvo. Sliding into the seat, she flipped over the battery and rolled the windows down to get a breeze flowing through the car. Tony followed shortly, reaching down to slide the seat back before he climbed in.

"Let's hit Minton's and Francia's first," Tony commanded imperially. He flipped Neva's radio from NPR to crappy pop music. She didn't even try to fight that battle.

"Why don't we just cut to the chase and go to Steinmart?"

"Because, grasshopper, that's not shoppin', that's gettin'." He nodded sagely, well as sagely as one can singing along to Cher, and she backed the car out of the driveway.

Three hours later at Steinmart, Neva stood in front of the triple mirror trying to explain to Tony why, exactly, she couldn't possibly buy a dress that started bright orange at the floor and lightened like a tropical sunset to peach at the neckline. Aside from the fact it had a full skirt, a *bow* for the love of God, and a crinoline underneath, it made her look like a Southern Belle who had escaped from some cheesy TV movie.

"No frickin' way." She toddled down from the stool she had to stand on to keep the dress from bunching on the ground, pulled the skirts up with her hands, and waddled back into the dressing room. Not that she should have bothered, since neither Mabel, the sales lady who had to be every day of 63, nor Tony would let her close the door to change. Luckily, Neva had no problems standing around in her underwear in dressing rooms while people yanked her in and out of clothes. Growing up, it was completely natural for someone else's mama to intercede and pluck at you and comment on your figure or the cut of your skirt when you went to Dillards or some other department store. Shopping was a group activity best planned for a year in advance.

"Look now, I'm not wearing anything that looks like an extra's costume from *The North and the South*." Mabel helped her off with the dress, and Tony shoved a couple more into the crowded fitting room.

The next dress she tried weighed approximately fifty pounds and was teal and gold with beadwork from hem to neckline.

"I'm going to collapse," Neva whined. The dress hit the fitting room floor with a decided thunk.

The red satin, forties-style dress with scalloped sleeves and a hemline to match wasn't bad.

"I won't be able to wear underwear." She smoothed the fabric over the line of her panties in front.

"Easy access," Tony said.

Mabel laughed uproariously. "He ain't wrong, honey."

"Next!" Neva flung the dress over her head with more speed than she felt she should have been able to muster.

She slipped into a black satin dress with beadwork at the bosom and across the hips in asymmetrical patterns. Just enough beading to look flashy, slightly trashy, and to cover underwear.

"This one." She pulled her hair back, looking at herself in the mirror.

"Baby, if you want this dress, all you gotta do is open your closet at home. You got it, you got about five of it. No." He was right. It was a variation on the same dress she always bought, but that was because it was the dress she liked. "I thought you were goin' crazy. Crazy people wear feathered dresses and pinecones on their heads."

"Feathers?" She considered it. Why not?

There were no feathered dresses to be had at Steinmart. However, Neva's first Ball dress of the season did end up being a sleeveless sheath with tassels, almost a flapper dress but sluttier. In red. The dress definitely said "buck wild" all over it. It was only after she got it home that she looked at the invitation to the Mystic's Ball and saw that it was a black and white formal. Formal meant ankle-length or better, and really not even ankle-length if you came from the right circles. Neva decided to keep the slutty flapper dress anyway and wear one of her black beaded ones to the Ball.

James Johnson called her just as CNN switched over from news to talk-show mode. Neva didn't mind the break from pretty talking heads who didn't so much talk as coo and yammer.

"Hello." She cradled the phone between her chin and shoulder, flipping through random video channels and home renovation shows.

"Vacation?" He sounded less than convinced.

"Well, some time off anyway." She wasn't sure where this was going, but it couldn't be good.

"Your sister called me." His tone rang tired, worried.

Neva sat up abruptly, grabbing the phone in her right hand. "No, she did not!" Nadia had really crossed the line.

"She did too. She says you need to see a professional. Is there something I'm missing? Because I thought you were just exhausted from work." He paused. "Is there something else?"

Neva thought about confessing to him, explaining about the weird images in her bathroom mirror, the hollow longing she felt for a lake she'd never really seen, the strange dreams of the Welsh boy from the pub. But she also knew how insane it all sounded. "Just exhaustion. Nadia's overreacting. Like that's new."

James had heard years' worth of Neva bitching about her sister's over-zealous micromanagement of everyone else's life. "If you say so." He let his words fade at the end, prompting Neva to speak up if she wanted.

She didn't. "Were you worried about me?" The words emerged playful and joking. James wanted to be set at ease, so he was.

"No more than when you decided to become a shut-in and work from home. Who in their right mind elects to live in Mobile?" His laughter ran down the line, and Neva let herself smile along.

"No one in their right mind." And she was making a joke on herself, making light of everything, so James laughed harder. He couldn't see her collapsed expression of worry. She wasn't so flip that she wasn't concerned about her mental health, but her sister calling her work colleagues really was beyond the pale.

"All right, if you're sure you're okay, I've got a three-foot stack of paperwork to cope with. I'll give you a ring about Cardiff next week anyway." The Wales project was a go. They were still in the preliminary stages, though, breaking the land and casting around for talent.

"No sweat. Check you then."

"Bye, Neva." James hung up. She set the phone aside and fumed over Nadia's back stabbing. The thought of calling their mama crossed her mind, but she realized that would get her nowhere.

On the desk were two tickets to the Mystic's Ball the next night. She could really get back at Nadia by embarrassing her in front of her coworkers. Neva laughed to herself. Damn it, she didn't have a date.

* * *

Convincing Tony to do her hair took all of three words: "chicken and dumpling." One of the life skills she'd picked up along the way to being a self-sufficient woman was knowing how to cook. Cooking well wasn't some sort of a throw-back, domestic goddess credential in the New South. It was the continuation of what few traditions they had and could maintain in a remade world. All week folks ate nonhydrogenated margarine and steamed vegetables and skinless chicken breast, but on the weekends, people cooked. Casseroles and whole chickens done fifty gazillion different ways, greens and cornbread and peas and beans. All the old-fashioned, cholesterol-shock inducing, pork-centric food that had been developed through the centuries to pull the most calories out of the least amount of food for an impoverished, starving population just made you fat in the modern era.

Wearing a size fourteen was worth it for speckled butter beans with homemade pepper sauce and cornbread in Neva's estimation. She'd learned to cook from her aunts and great aunts and mama. She felt at home in the kitchen, comfortable, which was why she entertained mainly at her kitchen table, over food she set out and iced tea she made herself. One of the benefits of working from home was being able to put on a pot of greens in the morning and be around to make sure they didn't boil over.

In her fridge the night Neva went to the Mystics Ball was sweet potato casserole—with pecans and coconut, made by her mama—mustard greens with a ham hock, half a chicken she was planning to use for a casserole for church on Sunday, and chicken and dumplings she'd made a couple days before.

"You had this shit in here and you ain't even call me up?" Tony was a fan of chicken and dumplings, as were many who were raised on it. Neva had her Great Aunt Myrtle's secret recipe; mainly the secret recipe called for the water in the dumplings to be ice water and the broth to have a bit of turkey in it.

She heated the chicken and dumplings up on the stove in one of her pea green Le Creuset pots. Some things couldn't be microwaved. Really, Neva hated the microwave in general. She thought somehow the radiation made the food taste weird. Especially chicken.

"I forgot." Clicking the gas on the burner on, she realized she'd been so distracted going nuts that she'd become even more of a hermit than usual. She thought back and it dawned on her that she'd only eaten with Tony and Jay once in the past two weeks, at the barbeque. Normally, they had supper together at least four times a week.

"If you were anyone else, I'd think you got a man in your life. A back-door man." Tony clattered around behind her, getting all of his hair-doing gear in order. Her grandmother would spit turpentine if she knew Neva allowed hairbrushes and curling irons to touch the kitchen table. She'd probably spray the whole house down with bleach if her geriatric arms could hold the gallon jug high enough. "So, you got a married man?"

Neva stirred the dumplings, smiling. She could see out the window above the sink and to the left of the stove. Her pink clematis shook and heaved and a squirrel ran out of the foliage, hopping on the ground and darting up the oak tree in the backyard.

"Yeah, and he's really famous, so I can't tell you squat." The broth in the pot began to boil, and Neva used a wooden spoon to make sure the dumplings didn't stick to the bottom.

"Ooooooooooooh, is he fine? I bet he has black hair." Tony spoke with a full mouth. Neva's money was on the red velvet cake sitting on one of her Aunt Tilda's crystal plates in the fridge. Neva wasn't a huge fan of red velvet cake, but Aunt Tilda had it in her head that it was Neva's favorite, so she made it every single time they saw each other. Luckily, it never went to waste.

For a second, Neva paused, thinking about Tony's comment about black hair. Here was an opening to tell someone about her dreams, about the weird visions and odd happenings.

"Don't burn my food, woman!" And in a rush of flailing hands and the clattering of Fiestaware, the moment was undone. Tony dished up his own food while Neva went to pick through her dresses to see which one Tony hated the least.

Tony, however, had other plans. He appeared at her shoulder carrying his bowl of dumplings cradled in his huge hand on an alligator-shaped potholder. "I think you should find some kinda goth charity and make a donation."

Neva rolled her eyes. "Not everyone can be a walking carnival billboard." She shoved a couple bags with dresses inside around in her spare closet.

"You saying I look like a good ride." Somehow he could deliver lines like that totally deadpan.

Neva cracked up, falling into the dresses a little. "Oh my god, I totally walked into that."

"So, who's your date, the mysterious, married, celebrity with black hair and dimples?" Tony plopped down on the daybed in the spare room. She didn't see him, but Neva knew he plopped by the sound the springs under the mattress made.

"Ok, so I'm predictable. I like black clothes and men with black hair." She felt sort of defensive for no real reason. There was no crime in being consistent.

"Honey, you're not predictable. Predictable people

don't have their sisters running around trying to convince everyone they've gone around the bend. Or before that that you had epilepsy. I thought that was trying too hard, transparent, like her addiction to fashion television. She's taken that whole 'don't wear black and colors combined' a little much to heart." He kept on prattling, but Neva stared through the clear, plastic bags at her formal-wear, thinking about Nadia trying to have her committed. She felt a tightness in her face and heard a slight roaring in her ears that signaled that her blood pressure was way up.

"Now don't go havin' a stroke." Tony grabbed her by the upper arms and shoved her towards the daybed. She glared up but allowed him to manhandle her. "You won't get your petty revenge on Nads if you stroke out and end up with a gimpy, slack skin thing happening on one side of your face. We need to focus."

Neva kept glowering, but Tony was absolutely unfazed. He grabbed a couple bags out of the closet and tossed them on the bed. Neva untied the knots in the bottom. Under the rustling of plastic, she could almost hear music. She glanced up at Tony, but he was busy rummaging around in the shoe boxes on the shelf above the hanging clothes.

"Even if your wardrobe is uninspired, you got some serious shoes, woman." He grabbed a box of Versace heels with an ankle strap. She'd gotten those in Brussels last year. Being a couple of seasons out of date really didn't matter in Mobile. Most people thought she was lying when they asked what kind of shoes she was wearing and she said Versace or Jimmy Choo or Prada. She was used to that. Her shoes weren't for other people anyway. They were her one real indulgence just for her.

"What're you wearing to Osiris?" Tony rummaged through the bags looking for something he found to be least frumpy or offensive. The Osiris Crew was the gay and lesbian Mardi Gras society.

"How about that flapper dress?" Usually she went with the crowd and wore a tux—one she'd actually bought just for the occasion several years before, all the time hoping she'd get other opportunities to wear the suit. She really sort of liked it.

"Bingo! Give the girl a moonpie!" Unrolling a black satin, floor-length gown beaded at the arms and hem, with a low scooped neck with red beads, Tony gave the dress the once-over. "Are these beads apples?"

"Yeah, I bought it a few years ago from a trunk sale. I thought I could use it for a Halloween costume or something."

"Are you kidding? You're the snake in the Garden, honey. Put it on, let me see." He shook the dress at Neva. She felt uneasy, but took it from him. The tiny red apples shone in the incandescent light in the bedroom.

Neva sat in her kitchen in her bra and panties, wrapped in a towel while Tony did her hair.

"You gonna take a taxi?" He was asking her if she wanted a drive, which was sweet considering how bad the traffic downtown was going to be.

"Yeah, if I can get one." She smiled as he tugged on her hair a little harder than as necessary.

"It ain't no thang if you want me to drive you. You get a mask today?"

"No, I've got about fifty. I'll just wear one of the old ones." Buying a mask was a whole episode, and there was no way she was going to try to do it in the middle of Ball Season when anything good was long gone, tourists and kids packing the shops and being hollered at by the shop owners.

"You should wear that snake one from a couple years ago." Neva knew he meant to match the apple theme, but she thought the green and black of the mask would probably clash with the dress and the bits of red beading Tony was pinning in her hair.

"I'll see." She was lulled by the rhythmic tug and stroking in her hair, fading out; the boy, March, appeared in her mind, sitting under a tree with his head down over what could have been a harp or a washboard.

Tony droned on about his azalea bushes and the infestation of what she would have sworn he said were pixies.

By the time her hair was twisted and bound into a complex system of beadwork and pins, Neva was rethinking the whole Ball-crashing event. She didn't really feel very much like annoying Nadia and ruining her night anymore. Mainly she felt like lying on the couch and trying to find some period piece on PBS or BBC America and eating banana-split Blue Bell ice cream in peace.

Tony had gone back over to Jay's to find some "coup de grace" that he said he had, and Neva was left to her own devices to pick through her various Mardi Gras masks. She kept them in long, flat, white waxed cardboard boxes nestled under her spare bed. Each delicate mask was wrapped in tissue paper and cradled in bubble wrap, each one a story unto itself. There was a bright yellow canary and black feather mask with upturned eyes and a slanted mouth from the Striper's Ball three years before. The next shone in iridescent brown and cobalt blue, peacock feathers standing a foot high over the eye holes. There were three similar ones in white feathers, one with turquoise beading, one with black, and the last with pink.

She unwrapped and rewrapped each mask, settling it back into a new position in the box, to be found again next year, the memories sliding against each other, cross pollinating and eliding through time into the myth of her life. Her fingers searched under the tissue, and she pulled out another bundle. The construction of feathers and beads was unfamiliar to her. Black raven feathers swooped around the eye holes, flying away from the mask to extend over the sides at least four inches from the cheeks and all around the top. The eyeslits stared out large and round, big enough that Neva's entire eye would be visible, brown with black lashes behind the jet black mask. Jet beads lined the bottom of the demi-mask where it ended above the mouth.

The mask was unfamiliar, but she was used to that. Sometimes her sister's or her mother's possessions would get jumbled together with hers. Shoes and clothes and jewelry, all of similar sizes and tastes escaped to the wrong closets and jewelry boxes. But black on black wasn't her mother's style, nor her sister's. That didn't mean anything, though. Her mama bought odd gifts constantly, forgetting to give them properly then stashing them in the home of whomever they were meant for. Neva would open a drawer and find a new set of maple spoons, walk in the bathroom and find a whole set of Philosophy makeup, stumble over a statue in the living room.

She pressed the mask to her face. It smelled like paper and dust and something else she had no name for.

"You got a new mask?" A voice said behind her.

Neva turned, the mask pressed to her face, and looked up at Tony through the holes, no small feathers obscuring her sight, just a clean line of leg until she tilted her head back and back to look up at his smiling face, his grey eyes. She sensed tension in him, worry, fear; she knew it was for her.

Neva dropped the mask from her face, and all she saw was Tony smiling down at her, a brooch in the shape of a perfect, red apple sitting in his huge palm.

"I got this at a flea market up in Huntsville years ago. On a lark. It's crystal." When she didn't reach out for it, he turned and pulled the plastic up on her gown. He fasted the brooch on the collar of the dress, up high almost on the shoulder.

"Come on, girl, let's get your face did." Leaning back down, he stretched out a hand, and she reached out her own and placed her hand in his. The odd, slippery stasis she'd felt drifted off on the timbre of his laughter and smell of his deodorant.

"Nothing too Phyllis Diller." She laughed as he shoved her into the kitchen.

"I know you didn't just say that." But he was laughing, too.

Neva stood on the front porch of her house sweating. Her black satin bra was soaked through, and she knew by the time she got to the Civic Center she'd be indecent. She could see the crystals in her hair and on her dress, and especially on her brooch sparkling in her reflection from her front windows.

A neighbor passed by, waving, walking his dog, fake cat-calling. She waved back with her mask. She held her dress up off the porch in her right hand, along with her shoes. On general principle she refused to wear her precious shoes for standing around and waiting. They were sitting down shoes, showing off shoes, maybe strutting shoes, not standing for very long shoes.

Finally, the taxi pulled up, and she bent down and slid the strappy Prada heels on. She held up her dress with both hands as she negotiated, the fabric heavy and slick in her hands. The driver actually got out and opened her door for her. She laughed as he winked.

"Civic Center, I guess?" He was older, rotund, wearing a Mobile Bay Bears t-shirt and shorts. Neva often wondered what it was about fat men wearing shorts in the most inclement weather, as though once a man hit a certain maximum density his lower legs could no longer be affected by weather. Mobile in February wasn't the coldest place on earth, but the guy sounded like a native—so 48° was damn cold for him. Still wearing shorts, though. Neva sighed to herself.

He rounded the back of the car, getting back in with a bounce of the tires and tilt to the chassis, and cranked up the air conditioning.

"Where's your date?" One of the things that transplants to the South often never acclimated to was the sort of nosy brusqueness the natives employed with a smile and a nod. There were topics that were never spoken of, and that could be a minefield, but aside from those sorts of cultural taboos, strangers felt no compunction asking direct questions of a very personal nature.

"I haven't got a date." She wasn't embarrassed to say that, not like she would have been when she was younger.

"Your husband in jail?" He eyed her in the rearview. Neva laughed with a bright spark of true amusement. She had no trouble seeing why he made that leap of logic: it was damned common in the deep South.

"Nah, he's working offshore." This was her standard lie when dealing with people who were too persistent about her having a husband. Alabama was not New York City, and the dream of white picket fences, eighty-thousand dollar weddings with eight bridesmaids, and a well-groomed troop of offspring was still alive and kicking. Neva was used to every person she knew trying to fix her up. In the last five years, as she approached Old Maid status, she lied and said her husband worked on the oil rigs out in the Gulf. It was a hard job, but it paid well, and the men were usually gone six weeks at a time.

"Pretty girl like you, surprised he could hack it," he smiled again. Neva was starting to feel uncomfortable. The driver was taking Dauphin, which was on the wrong side of Government Street from where they needed to go. The car slowed and got wedged into the barely flowing molasses of weekend partiers out early to hit the bars between Cathedral and Bienville Squares.

The driver stared at her steadily in the rearview, and Neva became increasingly uneasy. She dug into her bra—purses were banned from sitting on or under tables at the Ball in one of the many ridiculous bylaws they flaunted with pride—and pulled out a twenty for the driver. She flung the door open on Jackson Street and stepped out onto the curb. The driver hollered at her, but she ignored him. A clutch of college kids pressed against the cab, yelling into the open door at the driver to take them to West Mobile.

Even so early on a Thursday night, Dauphin and Jackson were swarming with drunk and getting-there youth. The bars lining the streets were thumping with megabass and bedecked in green and purple and gold for Mardi Gras. Neva wove between the bodies, holding up her skirt and fretting for her poor shoes. She was only about five blocks from where she needed to be, but she hadn't worn a watch. The window to get into the ball was only twenty minutes. The Mardi Gras Krewes were insanely persnickety about what times guests and members could enter the facility. She'd left her house in plenty of time to get in, if she were taking a car. However, for how long it would take her to walk there in four inch heels—it wasn't looking good.

A crowd blocked her progress on Conti Street and she did her best to weave through them. She ended up working her way closer and closer to the building along the road, to the point where her elbow and arm brushed against the plate glass of the front window. She glanced up from the pavement, which she'd kept an eye on to make sure her dress wasn't touching the nasty pavement, and saw a dive shop she didn't remember. The crowd undulated around her, turning her slightly to the side so that she faced the window of the scuba store fully.

The front display was a floor to ceiling salt water tank. Coral fans waved and tiny schools of tropical fish swarmed in glowing purple and translucent white. Some kind of parrot fish slinked by, dorsal fin wagging placidly. Neva looped her skirt up high in her left hand, tucked her mask into the neckline of her dress, and pressed her right hand against the glass of the storefront. Bubbles floated from an aerator on the bottom of the tank in a spiral pattern, up . . . up. . . . to break the surface of the water and allow the oxygen into the amalgam of the salt water. The sounds of the sidewalk—screaming and singing and drunken antics—faded to a bright, smooth stillness.

The surface of the water skittered in tiny wavelets. She could hear the far-away chiming, music like a template for what music once was. Staring into a static place in the tank, free from fish or seaweed or movement, Neva looked beyond the water, beyond the moment. She was standing at a lake surrounded by trees. Clouds floated across the reflective surface, transversing from side to side in elongated representations of themselves. Neva drew in a long, stuttered breath, tasting pine and clean air and humidity.

The crowd surged against her, pressing her into the glass hard enough to bruise. But she laughed all the same. Because she knew where the pond was. She knew exactly where it was and how to get there.

CHAPTER THREE

NEVA WOKE UP the morning after the aborted Mardi Gras Ball and rolled out of bed hungry and ready to take this whole hallucination business head-on. She wandered into the kitchen, fed the cats, and made herself some toast. She realized that by giving in to the weird visions in her head, she was really jumping over the line from sort of strange to full-on mentally unstable. A sane person maybe had visions—hey, it could happen!—but only serial killers and religious zealots acted on them. That second possibility gave her some pause as she ate her breakfast and sipped her coffee.

Could people have visions that were sent from some place else? A lot of people seemed to believe in it. Why Joan of Arc and not Neva? Aside from the whole saint thing. But was Joan a saint and therefore had visions, or was she a saint only because she did? Neva jumped into the shower and got dressed wondering about that.

Dog River was about a half-hour's drive to the north. Neva listened to Morning Edition on NPR as she drove. She thought about the pond on her grandparents' property and why she was so sure it was the same pond as in her dreams, visions, whatever. That seemed to indicate she had some kind of mental illness, since why would some supernatural something send her visions of a catfish pond? But as she pictured her dream in her mind, she could see the familiar dip of the shore and the pine trees she'd seen hundreds of times in her life.

Neva didn't get to canoe as much as she had as a kid, but she still knew the area around her grandparents' fishing camp damned well. She'd spent every weekend of her youth fishing and canoeing and tooting around in her Pawpaw's little outboard motorboat, trawling around with no intention, just loving to be outside.

She parked her car in the gravel driveway of her grandparents' camp. The humidity from a microburst thunderstorm clung to the ground, turning the afternoon heavy and slow. The air wrapped around her, tugging her from the air conditioning and leather of the Volvo and out into the sharp tang of mud and pine and brackish water. She slammed the door behind her, not bothering to lock it.

All she could hear so far up the Dog River was frogs and birds and wind in the trees. Pocketing her keys in the loose jeans she was wearing, Neva headed for the little pig trail that wound through the pines and oaks on her grandparents' property, over swampy ground and pine needles, away from the river and toward a series of spring-fed ponds.

The sound of her boots on the damp ground rattled and clomped in her own ears, far too loud. In the distance, she heard the familiar chiming. It didn't come from the direction she was heading. She stopped for a second, wondering if she had mistaken the pond in her dream for the wrong one. As she held her breath and stood rigid, clutching a pine tree, the echoing of the chime silenced. She waited, still holding her breath and going slightly light-headed, but all she heard was the chattering of squirrels and the screeching of angry birds.

She shrugged it off, trying to erase a sense of unease. Her pulse spiked and her blood pressure rose until she felt like she could feel her heart beating in her eyes. Neva had never feared the woods, never had any reason to, raised on hunting and hiking and tree-climbing, but as she turned back to the pig trail, she had to admit to herself that she was scared. Leaves crunched under her feet, and the humid air filled her lungs.

The trail ended at a gap in the ring of saplings clustered around a small pond. It was probably only fifty feet across. The trees marched to the verge of the water, their greedy roots prodding right into the mud where water ended and earth began. Neva stood in the one break in the trees, just wide enough to accommodate her, and watched the white fluff of clouds skate across the pond, the heart-breakingly blue color of the sky reflected back like infinity.

A breeze picked up behind her, obscuring the ambient sounds of forest creatures and avian critters in a susurration of leaves and pine needles and branches shuddering and straining.

Jump. A broken voice like leaves underfoot crackled into her left ear. Neva whipped her head around, fear making her tongue feel twice its normal size in her mouth.

JUMP. The urgency, the pleading came through the strain and desiccation in the voice, and Neva's terror hit the point of mindlessness.

She turned back to the pond, the perfection of the endless sky still reflected without a single ripple breaking the mirrored surface. Across the water on the opposite bank stood a picture-book perfect apple tree, fruit bright red against the green of the leaves. Neva blinked and bit her lip. Taking a deep breath to steady herself, she stepped back, intending to run. As she picked up her leg to take a second step back, behind her she heard the brittle chiming. That scared her more. Between phantom chiming and a well-known pond, she chose the water.

Using her braced foot for leverage, Neva jumped in a standing dive head-first into the pond.

Her entire body seemed to breach the surface at once. Her eyes were closed for her dive, but when an odd sense of vertigo was erased by the shock of cool water on her panicked, flushed skin, her eyes popped open.

The reflex to scream almost overcame her sense of self-preservation. Below her, the dark to light to lighter gradient of sunlight through water glimmered. Above her, the grey to black darkness of deep, deep water stretched. She was turned around, somehow, and she did her best not to panic, her own body already rushing up to the surface, her backside first, her natural buoyancy tugging her to the light of day. The feeling was so odd, falling downwards and towards the surface at the same time that she forgot about screaming and tried to twist around, to flip herself right side up. This took more effort than she expected, especially since she seemed to be moving at a more than normal speed through the water. She had just managed to spin her body around when her head broke the surface. She gasped in air and pushed her shoulders out of the pond by pumping her legs and arms by treading water.

Gasping, heart still working overtime, Neva propelled

her body with firm breaststrokes away from the center of the pond. She had no idea how she'd gotten so far from the bank, and she really didn't want to think about how she'd scared herself into jumping into a pond because of imagined voices. The whole going-out-to-the-pond-to-begin-with thing she shelved for two a.m. reflection a few years in the future.

Her clothes weighed her down, her boots were full of water, making her progress to the bank exhausting. She was sweating and not at all chilled anymore by the time she hauled herself up the steep incline that dropped off precipitously about three feet from the bank. She collapsed between two trees that leaned over the water.

"Aaah ahhhhhhh aaaaaahhh, remove all your steel, child!" A crow landed on the toe of her boot, head tilting rapidly, swiveling and bobbing as he alternated looking at her from one eye and then the other.

"What?" Somehow that just popped out.

"Steeeel! Sssteellll! STEEEEEEL! Aaaah aah!" The crow beat its wings up and down to punctuate his point.

"What steel?" And again, Neva saw no other course of action other than to attempt to clarify the situation. If a crow talked to you, you at least owed it to the universe to respond.

"Chaaaaaaaaaange your cloooooooothes!" The crow pecked at the leather on her boot, hard enough for her to feel the reverberations up to her ankle.

"Change into what?" Neva looked around. Because . . . talking crow? There could also have been a hovering wardrobe of random couture. No wardrobe. The crow just pivoted his head back and forth, his brown eyes somehow condemning.

She was more scared of the bird than of the fact that she was obviously stark raving mad. Birds could peck out eyes or scratch off your face with talons. Neva was never much of a bird person. The crow looked like he knew that.

"AAAH!" He suddenly beat his wings faster, lifting up from the end of her foot, and swept away into the trees. Neva remained on the ground, dripping, becoming increasingly chilled, blinking.

She pulled herself up, the water in her boots squashing between her toes, her jeans chafing her clammy skin. Her t-shirt clung to her, completely transparent, showing her bright pink bra. Lovely. Sighing and castigating herself for being an idiot, she shoved apart a couple of saplings to make her way back to the pig trail.

Her clothes seemed to weigh as much as she did, making every step a struggle. Roots and brambles tripped her. She picked her way around the pond, holding onto one tree after another, like pressing herself against a wall after having too much to drink.

The pig trail remained elusive; about twenty feet directly ahead of her, she saw a flash of bright yellow. She turned, twisting between the thick stand of trees, aiming for what had to have been sunlight. The trees seemed to move further and further apart as she trudged toward the flash of color. The gloom decreased, the trees changed from pine to willow, letting in more and more sunshine, until Neva's foot touched down on what was obviously a path.

The path was not her pig trail. It didn't wind and switchback on itself. In a straight, well-groomed line, the path marched from where she stood to a break in the woods, ending in a bright arch just visible in the distance.

The willows bent toward one another overhead, their branches interlacing into a living canopy, but their fragile boughs still allowed sun to dapple the path in a constantly changing dance of shadows and leafy light shapes. Neva set her water-logged boots upon the path with great unease.

She reached behind her, to unfasten her hair, pulling it out of the knot on the back of her head and rewinding it, the familiar motions a sort of meditative routine, grounding her and calming her. A couple of strands got caught on her right earring, winding around the silver gypsy hoops she always wore. The negotiation of hair out of earring distracted her from the oddness of everything that had happened since she got out of her car in her grandparents' driveway. She shuffled down the path, wincing as she pulled out several strands of hair, and only tuned back in when she stood one step away from the break in the woods, right in the middle of the sunlit arch at the end of the path.

Before her stretched a massive field. It filled every direction from the woods to the horizon. Various flowers clustered together in little patches of pink-blue-lavender and red-violet-white, in unending variations, the entire field a rioting afghan of competing color schemes. The smell of all the flowers was almost suffocating—rose and hibiscus and orchid and wisteria—hundreds of floral and fruity smells all wrapping together into something even worse than Bath and Body Works with the air conditioning broken.

Neva coughed, a couple of jittering, stifled barks. The grass around the flowers was the bright, light green of the earliest leaves of spring.

A high-pitched screech began somewhere in the distance to her right. Neva cupped her hand over her eyes and strained to see what was next in this psychotic break. Another screech—in a different ear-splitting frequency—emanated from another direction. Soon that was joined by a third, then more and more.

Neva stuck fingers in her ears, her mouth dropping open as several brightly-colored streaks whipped towards her, bobbing around her head, fluttering around her torso, prodding at her, flapping transparent wings in her face.

"Oh my god . . . fairies!" Neva laughed, even through the increasing headache the fairy screams were inducing.

One of the creatures, a tiny figure in a dark blue tutu with lighter blue skin and almost white-blue hair, hovered right in front of Neva's face. The screeching ended abruptly. Several fairies darted around her—yellow, pink, scarlet—zooming agitatedly. They were each no larger than the palm of her hand, and her hands were not large.

The blue fairy puffed out her cheeks, planted her hands on her hips, and pointed a tiny finger at Neva's face.

"You did not obey the crow, concubine of Mabon!" Her booming voice filled the field. Her pronunciation, with full, rounded vowels—like a British stage actress, gravitas in the consonants—forced Neva to pay attention.

"What?" Neva figured that had worked with the crow, why change it up?

The fairy beat her wings in what Neva took to be a threat. The ridiculousness of it all suddenly made Neva giggle. Once the laughter started, she couldn't hold it inside. Her laughter spilled out of her, bright and baffled and huge.

The fairy's imperious expression crumpled into one of resignation.

"You are no different from the others, human. You kill with a smile on your lips and amusement in your heart." She fluttered back slightly.

Neva wiped tears from her eyes and tried to frame a query about the fairy's comment, but she just shrugged. The screeches began anew. Worse. Neva looked down at her feet, where some kind of chaos had begun. A purple fairy alighted on the toe of her boot and instantaneously began to crumble in on herself, her skin blackening in rings and tendrils, her wings breaking off, her fluttering tutu catching fire. The fire spread to her flesh in a flash, and the fairy burnt out, ash dropping onto the leather of Neva's boot and the neon green of the grass.

Then a second fairy, pink this time, hovered too near Neva's boot in her frenzy to touch the ash of her fallen friend, and she blackened and turned to ash just as swiftly, just as horribly.

Neva raised a hand to her mouth, casting her eyes around for the blue fairy. She could no longer tell one from another, in their anger they swarmed around Neva's face, reaching out to scratch her with tiny fingernails and kick at her with miniscule feet. Neva futilely batted at them as she turned and stepped back into the archway to the woods. As soon as she stood between the entwined willows, the fairies fell back. They wove between one another, bobbing and diving, some screeching louder and louder and others chittering angrily.

She stood like that, watching the fairies freaking out, until she was freezing cold in her wet clothes. A vague sense of guilt hovered over her. She had no idea what had happened to the fairies, but she felt like crap about it nonetheless.

Turning her back on the granny-square glory of the fairies' field, Neva started back down the path in the woods in the opposite direction. She was not surprised when the place she stepped onto it was no longer the beginning. It stretched out in a straight line from the arch leading to the fairies down to another glimmer of sunlight in the far distance.

Neva sighed. She was cold, tired, and really flipping confused. She was either dreaming or crazy, and that just wasn't as reassuring as she wanted it to be. She trudged down the path, trying to figure out what would happen if she encountered something more threatening than fairy fury. What type of internal logic did this place function with? Was it what she made it up to be? Did she define the rules and therefore have the chance to vanquish whatever threatened her just with her mind? Did she have to really believe she was able to vanquish something in order to be able to?

Neva couldn't answer any of her own questions, so to keep the panic at bay, she switched to trying to remember how to knit the heel of a sock. Focusing on the mundane was a form of meditation that she'd learned in order to overcome her fear of flying. Don't let your mind spiral away thinking of what-ifs and worst-case scenarios. Instead, think of the most tedious and banal topic you can.

She began to sing to herself—Jimmy Buffet's "A Pirate Looks at Forty."

And she thought about how much she hated to knit, really. What was the point of knitting when you live some place that has no winter?

Neva decided she'd tell her mother to stuff it with the knitting. From then on, Neva would be knit-free.

"You are a strange creature, truly." An old man's voice, threaded through with vibrato, startled a scream out of Neva, interrupting her singing and musing.

She swept her head from side to side, looking for a human figure somewhere near her. Instead, her pulse trying to jump out of her neck, she saw the looming figure of a buck. His rack tugged small branches from trees as he broke out of the undergrowth. He was at least a twenty-point buck, the largest deer Neva had ever seen.

He shook his head, leaves and bark flying off his

antlers, then turned his face towards her. Her breath caught.

"Have you ever seen the ocean, child?" The deer's mouth didn't move, but she didn't hear him speaking in her head either. He was definitely verbalizing, but how, she couldn't figure out. Telepathy? She stared, oddly terrified. "Do I frighten you?"

The deer blinked. He was too large to fit onto the path, keeping his hindquarters hidden in the brush. He was at least the size of a caribou.

She nodded at him.

The deer blinked slowly again.

"You have seen the ocean; I can see its reflection in your eyes." He paused shaking his antlers again. "You need not fear me, child. I am no threat to you."

She wasn't really reassured, considering this was a magical talking deer who could crush her with one hoof.

"You killed the fairies because the crow never explains himself. What can one expect from a bird?" The deer snorted—the closest thing to a normal, deer-like sound he had made yet.

Neva couldn't see how she had killed the fairies.

"Your boots, child, they have steel rings through which the laces twine. Steel kills fairies." He blinked. "Many things kill fairies." He didn't sound like much of a fan of fairies. Which was odd, considering he appeared to be a mythical creature himself. Maybe there wasn't much solidarity amongst the magical communities.

"Why didn't the crow just tell me that?" Her jeans also had a steel alloy zipper and rivets. Her watchband was steel.

"He is a crow." The deer lowered his head, shaking it in what Neva took to be disdain.

"Am I in a coma?" Neva thought that was the least horrible of all the options.

"I know not what this coma is, child, but if you mean 'Are you a figment of my imagination?' I promise you I am not. You humans always think other creatures were created by you and your imaginations. The hubris would be amusing if it weren't so frightening." He snorted again. Neva saw agitation in the action, and she decided to just shut up about the whole crazy thing.

"Can you help me?" Normally, Neva would have never stooped to asking random talking animals for aid. However, she was well past normally.

The stag stepped back slightly into the woods, his front legs pawing the path. "Since you ask me for aid, I will give you more than what I am bound to offer you if you had not asked."

She wasn't sure if he was pleased or shocked or what. The motivations of magical deer were beyond her.

"If you follow this path to its ending, you will come to a tree bedecked with many pairs of scissors. Pick ones small enough to fit into your hair when restrained. Pick only golden scissors." He and pawed the ground once for what Neva assumed was emphasis. "Across from the tree of scissors will be another tree with a hollow trunk. Inside this hollow tree you will find clothing more suitable than that which kills."

"Should I trust you?" She had no idea why she asked him that, or why she expected an honest answer.

"Above all things, trust in thyself, child." The stag bobbed his head again, pawed the ground once, then leapt suddenly, impossibly high for his bulk, and disappeared into the trees.

"Huh." Neva started walking again. She hustled this time, the promise of dry clothing pushing her almost into a jog. She no longer sang to herself. She kept alert, scanning the trees in case some other bizarre creature leapt out at her and sent her on a quest after golden fleece or the Mad Hatter. All she saw were bright green grass snakes. They didn't speak. Maybe because she didn't talk first.

The length of the path seemed to somehow fold up on itself, because in less than ten minutes she stood next to an oak tree with a thousand pairs of scissors swinging from its boughs. Each pair shone in the light through the archway out of the woods, gleaming silver and brass and gold in the edge of the gloom. Neva surveyed the inexplicable tree. She pivoted on her heel and strode across the path to search for the hollow-trunk clothes tree. The scissors could hang on a second, but she absolutely had to change her wet clothes right now.

The hollow tree was something out of *Winnie the Pooh*—a gaping, oval gap yawned from the ground up to a few inches above Neva's head. A light shown from inside the tree. A breeze blew through the living leaves and branches as Neva tentatively stuck her head into the trunk.

She laughed, utterly delighted, and stepped inside.

The trunk of the tree was a huge round closet. The warm yellow light originated from a candle chandelier that seemed to hover in mid-air above her head. The floor was living wood. Clothes were strewn all over the floor, as though a pack of crazed teenagers had picked through the place looking for something to wear for picture day. However, on second look, Neva realized there were no hangers, no racks. The clothes apparently lived on the floor. She peeled her shirt off, tossing it across the room to land in a pile of other items. She kicked her boots off, then toed off her socks. Her jeans came next. She used a hideous puke green shirt to dry herself off. She peeked around in irrepressible paranoia and finally divested herself of her bra and panties. She wasn't about to get into dry clothes with wet underwear on.

Naked, she knelt on the floor and began pawing through the huge piles of clothes for something to wear. Saris, scarves, crinolines, muumuus, thigh-high boots, several single socks, a cloche hat, hot pants. No jeans or t-shirts. She scooted over to a new pile and started digging. Almost immediately she found a pair of boy-leg panties and a matching bra—both pea green—in her size. Apparently magic could produce underwear sets—she didn't complain. The cotton felt soft, and the clothes were oddly warm, like they had just come out of the dryer, when she put them on. After pulling out a hot pink catsuit and three pairs of yellow corduroy pants, Neva got bored and settled on a Pakistani-style tunic with matching loose pants—black with gold embroidery.

She pulled on the clothes. They were loose, comfortable. She reached into the next pile of clothes and snatched up a golden, knitted shawl—it felt like cashmere—and wrapped up all the other pairs of panties and several shirts and odds and ends in the wool. She knotted the ends of the shawl and then tied it all up so she could slide her arms through the holes like the straps of a backpack.

When she turned to the opening of the trunk, she saw a pair of shoes sitting right where she'd stepped into the tree. She walked over, and, naturally, the cross between ballet flats and moccasins fit her perfectly. They were black.

"Thank you," she said to no one in particular as she stepped back out of the tree into the woods.

She felt strange, a combination of distant and confused and oddly relaxed. Neva strode over to the scissor tree. The scissors knocked together in a fluttering breeze, sending an oddly familiar chiming through the woods. Neva stopped in her tracks, listening to the music of the scissors, her entire body covered with gooseflesh. The tree sang to her and she knew without a doubt that it had always been inside her mind somehow.

She shut out the terror. She was going to be the heroine of her own story, and she was not about to let some inanimate objects frighten her like some girl in a horror movie. She approached the tree, scanning the branches for a pair of golden scissors small enough to fit into the knot in her hair. Most of the scissors nearest her appeared to be silver. She picked her way over the roots of the tree until she was standing with her back directly to the arch out of the woods. By standing on the tall knuckle of a tree root, she could just barely reach the points of a pair of tiny golden scissors.

She stood on tip-toe, her arm stretched all the way up, and leapt slightly, her fingers coming all the way around the blades of the scissors. Her weight tugged the scissors free of the branch on which they grew. Neva stepped down off the knuckle of the tree and walked toward the sunlight, examining the scissors in her palm. They fit perfectly in the palm of her hand. The gold had been worked so that the loops of the finger holes were two twisting figures— one a deer and the other a pig. The blades were embossed with curlicues and symbols that Neva didn't recognize.

Neva stepped out of the woods while firmly lodging the scissors in the knot of her hair. She didn't even have time to assess her environment when the ground began to roil and leap under her feet. She had a chance to register that she had come out of the woods on the apex of a hill, how- ever, because soon she was rolling down the slope of it.

"I'll be goddamned!" Neva rubbed the back of her head, fuming. When was this going to either change to the fantasy world where she was married to George Clooney . . . or she woke up in her bed?

"Odd choice of words." Neva recognized the voice that answered her. She sat up all the way, body protesting the bruises and scrapes she'd accumulated falling down the hill. She was almost to her knees when the ground began shaking again. Falling on all fours, Neva braced herself on her hands as the grass under her seemed to fling itself at her.

The earthquake abated, the ground still not steady, but steady enough for Neva to sit back on her heels and look around the gully for March. She patted her hair to make sure the scissors were still in place and shrugged the makeshift backpack more firmly onto her shoulders. Oddly, she hadn't lost either the pack or the scissors in her tumble.

"Hey!" Neva shouted when she finally spotted March, leaning with his ankles and arms crossed against a huge, grey stone fifty yards or so from her.

She appeared to be in some sort of ravine. Rising in front of her was the hill she'd fallen down. Behind her was another, steeper hill. Down the ravine in one direction several large boulders stuck out of the ground like chipped teeth. In the other direction the headwaters for a tiny stream began; the stream widened further down the valley.

Holding on to the straps of her woolen pack, Neva picked her way over rocks and uneven ground toward the figure slouching on the dolmen.

The closer she got, the more surprised she became. In her memory, and even in her dreams, she remembered the boy as handsome—very handsome—but just one more beautiful boy in a world full of them. This man was incandescent, radiant. His thick black hair curled slightly, creating a tiny winged halo around his head. His lips, even pulled into a smirk, were the bright pink of the inside of a conch shell. His eyes turned up slightly on the outside edges, giving him an air of the exotic—the color of the clear water of the Caribbean, the aquamarine of the Byzantines, deep and multifaceted. His wide, square jaw was tipped with a slightly cleft chin. His nose, the indentation above his top lip, and chin cleft were all in perfect, symmetrical alignment.

Neva frowned. Perfect people always annoyed her more than anything else. They expected more for less, got their way without effort, just a luck borne of genetics. When he pushed away from the rock and took an insouciant step toward her—all hip swing and languid lift of his chin—she was even more annoyed by his height. He loomed over her, well over six feet tall.

"Did you get the scissors?" March wore some kind of Robin Hood-style outfit, but in black instead of bright green with a long-sleeved tunic that ended high on his thighs and tight pants tucked into knee-high boots. He had a quiver of arrows and a bow strapped to his back. He was broad as well as tall, probably two hundred and fifty pounds worth of looming self-assurance. She was not at all surprised to find him here in this weird world. It was the fact of recognizing it that made it strange, how the loops in her logic *didn't* concern her, that made her worry she was losing her mind.

"What scissors?" Neva tested the rules. Mainly she just wanted to jerk this guy around, but she needed to test the boundaries—to see if this world worked like a video game where you had to ask a set of specific questions before you could advance to the next stage. She wondered how many responses on her part would elicit the correct prompt from him.

March rolled his eyes and crossed his arms over his chest, taking a step back from menacing her with his height. His chin tilted down so that it rested on his chest, as he watched her through his eyelashes. "You have the scissors," he said finally. His accent was now Midwestern American, not Welsh. His voice had a pleasant, rough nap at the edges, straining around 'h's and 'i's.

"You must find two locks of hair: one pure gold, the other pure black. Then you must bring them back here, to me, to placate the worms beneath the ground who battle eternally." March proclaimed this with the sort of bored, by-rote tone that Neva associated with dinner theater and high school drama productions. She blinked at him.

"What happens if I don't?" She crossed her arms over her chest and glared up at him.

His smile spoke of secret things in the dark, of terrors too old to have names, of promises of destruction whispered as curses. Her whole body blushed hard, and she felt a rush of excitement she hadn't in a long time. It felt a lot like desire.

"That is not for me to say."

Neva didn't exactly run away, but only because the rocks made her step carefully.

Now, Neva'd had bad days. Days when the car stalled in rush hour traffic. Days when she started her period right before leaving for Cancun. Days when she accidentally insulted her boss's fiancé's sense of style.

But Neva was having a *very* bad day. She had murdered some fairies, gotten lost in Wonderland, decided she was completely insane, and the best conversation she'd had all day was with a talking deer. She needed a drink. Or to be sedated.

March, well, she didn't want to think about him a whole lot because she thought it was probably the most screwed up part of her day that she thought his whole evil-ing at her was just about the hottest thing she'd ever seen.

Why did he sound like he was from Ohio all of a sudden? Was it wrong for her to find someone barely twenty years old that fine?

Had the muscles in his arms really been rippling, or was that a hallucination?

The ravine widened out as the stream grew in size. Neva sat down on a rock under a tree and felt sorry for herself. She had nothing to eat. She must have missed the prompt where she got to find food. This made her bitter, and her blood sugar bottoming out made her nearly homicidal.

"Yooooooooou must find the hair," a thready voice bleated right above her head.

Neva sighed, but she looked up anyway. Clutching the lowest branch of the tree between his claws, an owl about the size of a robin sat perched just over her. His breast feathers were light brown, his back and wings darker brown with black pinions, and his eyes were ringed in cream. The owl blinked. Neva smiled despite herself. She blinked back at him. The owl skipped down the branch slightly, then back again to his original position.

"Yooooooooooou must find the hair." The owl beat his wings slightly.

"Why?" Neva did not like events being so out of her control. This whole, well, world seemed to work on training-wheels, everything followed some kind of pre-ordained pattern. But she hadn't ever heard this story. She had no template to work from.

The owl blinked a few times. "Tooooooooo stop the dragons."

"Why must the dragons be stopped?" If the owl could tell her one thing, maybe he could tell her more.

"Tooooooooooo release Mabon! WHOOOO WHOOOO!" He jumped a little, beating his wings excitedly and bouncing on one talon.

"Who is Mabon?" She wasn't exactly sure she wanted to release anyone. Who the hell knew what would happen then?

The owl settled down, cocking his head to the side. "The Eternal Yoooooooouth!" He beat his wings emphatically.

"Great, I have to beat this whatever it is or a kid dies. Typical." Neva couldn't have gotten the whole quest for the Holy Grail or something else that might be cool and also beneficial to *her*, no, she got the one with child murder and maybe a little more sacrilege than she was comfortable with. "Okay, fine."

She hauled herself up off the rock. The branch the owl perched on was about chest high. She reached out a tentative hand and motioned gently toward the bird. He blinked but didn't try to bite her. She took that as his permission. His feathers felt like solid water, slick and fluid under the backs of her fingers as she stroked his belly.

For some reason the bird allowing her touch made her laugh, genuine and real and thrilled. The owl nipped at her hand gently, making a soft coo. She took that as a sign that she'd molested him enough.

Neva waved to the owl as she started back the way she'd just come.

March was lying on the ground with his hands laced behind his head when she got back to the headwaters of the stream. He rolled to his side, one arm propping up his head, and the other pressed firmly in the grass by his belly when Neva approached him.

"You've given up already?" He laughed, the bitterness underlying it ruining the toe-curling beauty of his voice.

"Where do I get the hair?" Neva raised an eyebrow at him. People like him—pretty people with such tragic, ridiculous pain—made her ill.

March's laughter cut off abruptly, and he rolled himself to his feet. His hair in disarray somehow looked even sexier.

"What?" Somehow she'd shocked all the cynical languor out of him.

"I said where do I get the hair? The owl told me I have to get it. He didn't know where. So I'm asking you. Where. Do. I. Get. The. Hair?"

"Why are you asking me?" He ran a huge hand through his hair, and it magically fell into perfect, just-rolled-out-of-bed order.

"It's only logical that since you told me about the hair that you know how to get it. So?" She was beginning to lose her temper again. She was so hungry. And this guy was weird and pinged her all wrong. She wondered if she could get the scissors out of her hair fast enough if he tried to hurt her . . . if that's what they were for. Although she had realized immediately when March mentioned hair that the scissors were for that job.

"No one's ever asked me where to go before." He sounded shocked, confused, and she hoped that she hadn't just shot the entire storyline to shit by asking him to help her. He turned his back to her, reached down and picked up his arrows and quiver.

Neva stepped back reaching back into her hair.

But when March turned back around, his smile could have melted an iceberg. His teeth gleamed white and even—one incisor slightly chipped, like a flaw in a sculpture by one of the Old Masters to remind themselves that only God created perfection.

"Are you hungry?" He had deep, deep dimples in his pink cheeks when he smiled.

"If I eat here, will I be trapped forever?" Neva followed behind him, trying to step where he stepped, as he nimbly navigated the rocks on the ground.

"What do you think?" He looked over his shoulder at her, chuckling at her or to himself, she wasn't sure. Another twist of annoyance spiraled through her belly. She opened her mouth to tell him to go to hell when the ground began to pitch again. She got her hands out in front of her but still smacked her cheek against a rock when she fell.

March leaned down and picked her up. All the way up, with his hands under her arms, and set her on her feet again. He squinted at her.

"OW!" Neva yelled, glaring at March. "What the hell's wrong with you, idiot? Picking someone up by their armpits? That shit hurts!"

He reached out with his sleeve rucked down over his fingers, frowning. "How should I have picked you up, then? Tossed you over my shoulder?" He grabbed her chin, holding her head immobile, as he wiped at her cheek with his sleeve.

"Is that bleeding?" She hissed as the fabric abraded the skin further.

"Not too much. You shouldn't break your falls with your face. It's a shame to ruin it." He half smiled.

"Are you flirting with me?" His smile collapsed and his hard look reappeared. "Oh, you don't like getting shot down, huh? Well, screw you. You're behind me being here, right? Am I drugged?" She still didn't want to give up on the hope that she was hallucinating.

"You think I drugged you?" His hand dropped away from her cheek, and the hand holding her chin tilted her head back so he could look her in the eye. The nerve of him to manhandle her like that! Her anger overrode the fear that spiked up in a cold flare from the base of her spine. The vein by his right temple throbbed. Neva was beyond caring. She needed to eat and take ten ibuprofens and drink herself to sleep.

"Are you dangerous, Neva Jones? Do you know how to be?"

She was reaching into her hair for her scissors when he said it. His tone rang out devoid of sarcasm or hauteur, as though he was trying to take her measure. He dropped his hand from her face and stepped around her, following along the stream. She followed him after half a minute.

CHAPTER FOUR

AS THE STREAM turned to river, the valley widened and the rolling foothills developed into mountains. Neva watched the slope of the mountains grow steeper and steeper through the thickening trees until the woods became a forest and she could only see trees to the left and river and trees to the right. She followed behind March, unsure exactly why, other than it seemed the thing to do, as the footpath by the river became more of an actual road. The sound of water rushing over rock and the chirping of birds covered any noise March made, crunching gold and orange and red leaves under his feet.

The trees shouldered closer and closer together until the river was just a hollow roar beyond them and the scent of water was like outdoors on the back of Neva's tongue. The sunlight became triangles and rhombuses and fractals shifting over the ground and March's body. The gloom suited the surreal, hovering feeling that was lifting her out of herself. Neva's world condensed into hunger and the shifting of light over the glossy black of March's hair, the matte black of his clothing, the slick black of the leather quiver on his back.

She might have been tired from walking for so long, or she might have been weak from hunger, but little by little she slowed down and the distance between her and March grew with each step. The sunlight became dimmer, the irregular patches of bright yellow further apart and fewer.

"Are you hungry?" March's voice came from further away than she thought it should, and when she concentrated, she couldn't see him.

"I told you that already." Her blood sugar had bottomed out hours ago, and her anger hit her with no warning, zero to pissed in one second.

"There's hunger and then there's passing out." His voice snapped back at her, and his own anger made her smile. He was easy to annoy, and that pleased her in a childish sort of way.

She took a step toward where she'd heard his voice, to the left in the deep shadows of the trees. She heard a low "thwang" behind her and a whoosh near her head, and was shocked to get knocked down to the ground by a tree branch she didn't see. She spun as she fell and landed on her front instead of on her back. Neva sprawled in dead leaves and moss and brambles underneath the weight of wood and leaves and fruit from the branch March had apparently *shot off the tree*. In a series of swift movements, the weight was removed, a hand wrapped around her arm, and she was hauled to her feet. March smacked the front her clothes, muttering to himself and dislodging debris and dirt.

"If you'd just stood still, that would have had quite an

effect, dropping right at your feet, but no, you walk towards the man shooting an arrow right over your head."

He bent over her, his hair brushing her cheek, one hand holding her tight around her bicep, the other thwack-thwacking her tunic and pants.

She tugged away, flushing with embarrassment and annoyance. "What the hell are you doing? Get off me, you freak."

He stood back, but didn't drop her arm.

"I'm helping you." The inflection was off, half-way between a question and a statement.

"You're bruising me." Neva twisted her upper body so that his arm strained with her movement, and he finally peeled his hand away.

She could barely see him because he was blocking the light with his body, couldn't see his face at all. However, she could definitely hear him sigh, feel the release of breath on her face. March stepped back and bent to the ground. When he straightened, he pressed a smooth apple into her hand.

"If I eat here, will I be trapped forever?" She wasn't exactly sure she cared anymore, since it felt like her internal organs were about to start eating themselves, but she repeated her earlier question all the same.

"I guess if you're really hungry you'll find out." His tone held an edge, and she was pissed at him for being pissed at her. He had dropped a tree limb on her. She thought she was being pretty reasonable about that, considering that then he acted like the incident was *her* fault.

Her teeth broke the skin of the apple, and she forgot about March, about the pain in her right arm in five long stripes like the purpling shadows of March's fingers, about the cool twilight of the forest, about Mobile and her family. The apple tasted of quince and music and the fresh scent of rain in the country after ten lifetimes of drought. The second bite slid into her mouth with the freedom of all of childhood's wonder and promise, with the impossibly bright green of the first leaves of spring, with the promise of happiness beyond her comprehension. It wasn't just that she was hungry and the apple nourished her, there was something more to it, a drugging effect. The apple was both sustenance and Ecstasy at once.

She even ate the core.

When the taste of the apple was just a memory, Neva opened her eyes to find March watching her. He stood close enough that her immediate reaction was to retreat a half-step. His expression bled into the darkness, a parallelogram of sunlight floating over his face, illuminating an eye, the slope of his cheek, the corner of his mouth, but not giving Neva anything close to the ability to judge his mood. He scared her a little, made her uneasy due to their size differences and his already established mercurial moods.

He pressed another apple into her hand and wrapped his hand around her free hand.

"It gets darker and darker from here. I don't want to lose you." His voice sparked with laughter. She had no idea why he was laughing, but she also didn't care since she had another apple, and that was all that mattered in the world.

She let him tug her along, eating one apple after another until she was full and even the promise of the rapture of the fruit couldn't overcome the bloating of her stomach.

The total blackness of the woods really was more of an oppressive gloom once Neva's eyes adjusted. She could see skin—her free hand sticky with apple juice, her other hand lost in March's grip, the side of March's face disappearing into the darkness of his hair—and the ink-drawings of the outlines of trees.

"Where are we going?" she whispered, with the instinct of generations of humans cowering in the dark, fearing nothing specific and everything vague.

"Those things you whisper to avoid can see in the dark, so that's pretty pointless." March spoke in his normal tone, bored, haughty.

"Well, I'd prefer not to bring them from a distance, you know? Even if they could see us, that doesn't mean they're standing two feet away, but now I guess it's pointless, because you had to put me in my place." She wanted to tug her hand away and stomp off, but her better sense overcame that impulse. What use would stomping away be when she'd just have to stomp back and eat crow?

"You're moody." The amusement floated back into March's voice.

"*I'm* moody? You're like thirty-four flavors in one cone, Mr. Kettle." His grip tightened around her hand as she snapped at him.

"That one flew over my head." He laughed slightly, under his breath, and jostled Neva with his shoulder.

"Pot calling the kettle black? Baskin Robbins?" When he didn't respond, Neva shrugged. "Yeah, well, I guess demons or incubi or whatever you are don't get pop-culture programming."

"I'm not a demon." His voice was absolutely devoid of laughter.

"What are you, then?"

He didn't answer. She wasn't all that surprised, because that would have been far too easy. She suspected this was another one of those video game moments where she'd have to kick over a barrel accidentally or trip over something to move on to the next part.

She tried again. "Where are we going?"

"A little bit further." The bored tone had returned.

"That's the answer to 'how far are we going?' not *where*." He didn't say anything. "Fine, but if you're leading me to some lair to cook me in a big cauldron, I'm going to be pissed."

"If I was going to cook you and eat you, wouldn't I have just hit you on the head with a rock a long time ago or shot you with these arrows on my back?" He sighed as though her faulty self-preservation instincts were just too much to bear.

"How do I know what sort of internal logic works here? I did mention the talking animals, right? There's probably a specific order to the steps that have to happen in order for you to get to eat me." She no longer doubted the reality of this place. She kicked that around in her head a little. Probably the apples. They were drugged somehow or magical or . . . yes, she had really just posited that magical apples really were the explanation for something.

"You're smart." He said it as though it pleased him.

"Most men aren't so thrilled about that." She laughed for no real reason other than the truth of that.

"I could say I'm not most men, but it'd be pointless since it's obvious." He squeezed her hand.

"Except you did just say it." The laughter this time was directed at March. Oddly, he laughed along. As far as the strange creatures in this place went, he was shaping up to be less predictable than the talking deer.

The gloom began to dissipate, gradually becoming grey instead of black. March pulled her closer to him, and she noticed their path was obscured by a fallen tree . . . no, by a freaking huge tree root.

"Um." She really didn't have much to say about the tree root that was higher than she was tall, or about the tree it was attached to that seemed to be about the size of the Empire State Building.

March shoved her in front of him, right at the tree root, and she flinched, raising her hands up to protect her face from the pain of collision. Neva turned her head to cuss March out, and was glad her face was averted because suddenly the brightness around her blinded her and made her head hurt.

"Oh my god, what the hell?" She snapped her eyes closed and covered her face with her hands.

When Neva peeked through her fingers, she found herself in a field of waist high grass reminiscent of saw grass or sea oats, long, thin stalks tipped in tufts of bushy hairs. The sun shone high in the sky, at its apex. The field ended in the near distance at a high wooden wall.

"Where are we?" Neva asked March, who stood a few steps ahead of her running the palm of his hand across the white tips of the grass. His head was bowed toward the ground, his hair obscuring his face.

"In the Land of Magog." Abruptly, he threw his head back and laughed, as bright as the day around them and just as unexpected. "It's been a long, long time since I've smelled the sharp scent of the meadow grass beneath my boots or tasted mead in the halls yonder."

He sounded like someone from Dungeons and Dragons. Neva wasn't impressed, considering that for someone as young as he was a long, long time was probably a month.

"Is that where we're going?" She pointed at the wall, turning her head to see if anything lay behind them.

Nothing at all from horizon to horizon but blowing grass, them, and the wall.

When he didn't answer, just gave her a huge smile displaying his dimples and chipped tooth, she stepped around him and started for the wall. "How was I supposed to know to walk through a tree root?" She mumbled to herself. Honestly, that was impossible.

"You weren't. The root is a shortcut." March said from close behind her. His smile threaded through his words, and because he couldn't see her, she smiled in return.

"What's the long way?" Neva asked, finally, after several long moments of wading through the grass.

"More talking animals, beanstalk, you know, the usual." His teasing voice was low, meant for conspiracies, and Neva imagined if she was looking at him, he'd wink.

"How predictable. Y'all need some better clichés around here." As they approached the wall, Neva realized it had been further away than she'd thought, because she was judging based on assumptions on its size. The closer they came, the larger the wall appeared to grow. "Is there some sort of optical illusion at work here?" And why she thought that it was anything other than magic, she conceded to herself, was completely self-delusional.

"Sort of. I never thought about it." Neva turned to look at him over her shoulder, and he was still smiling, wide, open, huge, like he'd swallowed all the secrets of the universe with an orgasm chaser, and framed by the bottomless blue sky and green and white grass, he was beautiful in a way that bordered on criminal. Ruddy face and lipstick pink mouth, curling black eyelashes and his eyes half-closed in amusement, head hanging down, sort of cocked to the side.

He winked at her.

She laughed before she could stop herself. When she

swept her head around to watch where she was going, the wall loomed only about fifty feet away. She stood on the edge of the sea of grass, and one step farther toward the wall was a well-kept lawn. She tilted her head back to see the top of the wall. It was tall. She'd guess castle-height. The dark wooden beams bit at the sky with jagged tops. As she tried to decide which question to ask first, nine doors simultaneously opened all along the wall, and chaos erupted, huge people—giants—flooding out of the doors, all tripping over each other to scurry toward Neva and March. They were screaming at each other and flailing their arms, some dancing in little groups with ropes of material interweaving between them, others playing piped instruments, some just running flat out in various directions. The shortest amongst them must have stood ten feet tall to judge at a distance.

Neva blinked, considered stepping behind March, thought better of it and just stepped to stand hip to hip with him. His arm came around her back and settled on her shoulder. She almost shrugged him off, but his hip slid against her side and he folded himself down to kind of drape around her, projecting solidarity and familiarity in the face of this madness. He smelled like the outdoors, sap and spice and tang, reminding her of the taste of the magical apples, and she liked it.

They stood together, the grass blowing around them, as hundreds of, well, giants converged between them and the door in the wall. Neva watched them come, her mouth slightly open. They were dressed in tunics and dresses with no apparent distinction made for gender. Some women wore tunics and others loose, flowing dresses. Men wore ground-length, woolen dresses and some wore short tunics with loose-legged trousers. They weren't misshapen with huge noses and disproportionately long arms or hump-backs. They looked human, just super-sized, between ten and fifteen feet tall.

Neva squinted at March. "Beanstalks, huh?" Oh, he thought he was funny, a small smile twisting his mouth up. He shifted against her, heavy and hard with muscle. It was easy to be near him, made her feel special even though she knew his beauty had nothing to do with her at all. It was easy to be near him when he was *quiet*.

Another commotion rippled through the giants, the crowd splitting and gaping. In the breach formed by the large figures emerged a woman. She wore a crimson silk dress that didn't leave much to the imagination. No way could anyone wear underwear with that kind of slinky, clinging fabric. Her hair was half bound on the nape of her neck, the rest spilling over her shoulder in loose ringlets of towheaded blonde. Her cheeks were flushed almost as red as her dress, which in turn matched her bright bow of a mouth. Her neck was encircled by a heavy choker of rubies and emeralds. But the most spectacular aspect of her entrance were the white flowers that sprung from the ground as she walked.

"Greetings." She bowed slightly, giving them a perfect shot down the front of her dress. Neva doubted the glimpse of pink nipples and perfectly rounded breasts was for her. "You are honored guests in my father's house." Her voice rang out lighter than Neva would have expected for her size and sparkling with joy. Neva decided there was no point in immediately hating beautiful fairytale characters—they tended to have tragic life histories that made up for the insufferable snowy bosoms and naturally platinum hair, as she vaguely recalled. Neva wondered what March's beauty said about his own fairy-tale life.

Neva tried not to make eye contact with all the people

staring holes in her head from behind the woman who just had to be the princess in these parts. This took quite an effort because she was trying damned hard not to make eye contact with the princess herself, who kept smiling winsomely at a spot over Neva's head that was bound to be March's smiling gob.

"Thanks," Neva said, in a lame attempt to move this whole scene along.

"Since you accept my hospitality we can proceed to the Great Hall and dine!" The presumed princess stood back, clapping her hands together and laughing. More of her hair came loose and fell to frame her face. "It's been ever so long since guests came through the grass to seek out our hospitality." She paused, her smile growing larger, her cheeks dangerously red. "Ever so long."

That did not sound good in the least to Neva. Her brain coughed up a vision of a giant cauldron hung over a raging fire with Neva-bits sticking out of it, the princess with a colossal wooded spoon jabbing Neva's arm back into the boiling stew.

"Follow her," March bent and whispered in Neva's ear as the weird giantess practically skipped back through the parting crowd.

He had to move his hand from her shoulder to her lower back in order to propel Neva forward. She stumbled slightly, and several giants rushed forward to steady her. One almost broke her hand when he snatched at it to keep her on her feet.

"Um, thanks!" She did her best to keep the pain out of her voice over the misguided enthusiasm. The giant who had helped her wore a pleated gingham skirt and peasant blouse. His dark beard and hair were cropped close to his skin. He smiled down at her, pleased with himself.

"No thanks needed, darling!" The giant had a British

accent. Neva repressed the urge to sigh. Things were getting curiouser and curiouser, but Neva had never dreamed of being Alice.

March shoved her slightly again. "Just walk. I know the way."

"No, really, I'm shocked." Neva did as he said, though, because she really just wanted to get away from the crowd before they started "helping" her more. She cradled her hand against her belly.

March touched her elbow and leaned down closer to her ear as the walked in the path created amongst the giants. "Are you hurt badly?"

"I'll live," she snapped at him. His moods were too hard to read—sarcastic and unhelpful one minute, besotted with grass the next.

"I was just going to offer to fix it for you, but forget it," he snapped back.

Neva rolled her eyes as they passed through one of the gates in the wall. The gate itself was a high arch that Neva craned her back to look up at as they passed through. Oddly, the gate did not open up into a town. She looked behind her and saw the wall from the other side, stretching off into the distance in either direction. Giants flooded back through the open gates. In front of her was a stone bridge arching over a deep, wide river, and a flagstoned path led in a winding circuit to a rambling building made of brick and stone. The path was set in the same sort of well-kept grass as on the far side of the wall.

March and Neva stepped onto the path, the giants keeping some distance behind them.

"Okay, so this is weird." She looked through the open arches on the bridge at the river as they crossed it. "Cross-dressing giants?"

March glanced at her, his expression unreadable. "You

keep expecting everything to work like a story you've heard?"

His tone pretty much wrote CONDESCENDING in the air between them. Apparently he was going to stay with being angry with her for a while because she'd peed in his cornflakes by not allowing him to help her. She had to admit that he was right, though. She did keep expecting things to work like a fairytale, which—no matter how far-fetched—tended to have a certain inherent logic. Walls in the middle of nowhere and cross-dressing giants really didn't have any point. Which could, perhaps, be the point in and of itself. Why would magic have to have a reason or a pattern? She wished for a moment that she'd read more books about fairies, or at least had let James drag her to see those *Lord of the Rings* movies.

They walked in silence, and Neva saw that at the end of the path the blonde princess stood with a man outside the brick and stone building. As they approached, the man stepped away, striding purposefully to her and March. He was a strong, sturdy man, even for the giants, with black hair and a full beard. His long, dress-like tunic fell to his feet and was belted with a golden chain with links in the shape of boar heads.

"I didn't believe Olwen when she said one had come through the grass accompanied by you, my friend." The king bent and smacked March lightly on the back, rocking him on his feet and sending several arrows tumbling out of their quiver. Neva smiled as March bent to pick them up.

The king turned to Neva. "My daughter is . . ." He paused, his lined face forming a wry expression. "Doesn't always perceive things the way the rest of us do." He smiled, and his white teeth shown through his beard. So, the princess was dim. *Quelle surprise.*

The king patted her on the head, rattling Neva's teeth, and March smiled at her with apparent schadenfreude. "You are most welcome in my hall, most welcome indeed. I suspect we shall be fast friends, you and I." He smiled with such genuine bonhomie that Neva smiled back, glad to get a chance to experience the hospitality, feeling slightly guilty about the earlier mental imagery of the stew pot.

"I hope so," Neva responded.

March sighed next to her, too softly for the king to hear. Neva turned to glare at him. The king turned around, wrapping his arm around his daughter's shoulder. He looked back at March and Neva. "Come inside. Relieve yourself of your burdens and relax by my fire. We shall feast in your honor."

When he turned back to walk into the house, Neva glared at March. "What's your problem?" She hissed.

"Just trying not to get my hopes up." He gave her a pointed look that was substantially blunted because Neva had no idea what the point was.

"Yeah, whatever." She added the "go to hell" in her head. "Your cryptic pronouncements have lost their luster, sucker."

He tilted his head slightly, in what looked like an unconscious movement. A tiny smile produced a tiny dimple in his cheek. "Sucker?" The smile grew.

"Yeah, well, I censored myself in case any of those giants are kids and I can't tell." If Neva ever flounced, then what she did then could have been called such.

The house of the giants—and here Neva just assumed they all lived together in one massive house because that was the least reasonable thing, and she decided to from now on go with the opposite of what she'd expect—smelled of citrus and tobacco. The floor stretched away in every direction in a chaos of colorful tile. There was no pattern, just random colors conflicting with each other in spirals and splotches and random geometric shapes. The ceiling curved overhead, the apex hung with a chandelier glinting in gold. Behind Neva and March, the other giants flooded into the house, peeling away from the group to wander in little clusters and pairs away from them. Their laughter filled the cavern of the room, rebounding off the walls, wrapping Neva in reflected happiness. Her smile welded itself onto her face.

She glanced at March to see him shaking his head and smiling so huge his face looked like it ached. She bit her bottom lip to keep from commenting on how pretty he looked.

"It's impossible not to love them, you know?" March said with a shrug. Neva agreed.

On the other side of the huge room was a fireplace probably fifty feet high. The fire roared behind an elaborate screen decorated with scrollwork that Neva couldn't make out from so far away. Various groups of giants scampered about the room constructing tables out of modular parts, then lugged chairs to set at the tables, and then bedecked each of the several tables with multicolored tablecloths and linens.

"They like bright colors, huh?" Neva laughed to herself.

"Oh yeah. You're lucky it's not the Season of Hair Coloring." He started to laugh about halfway through the statement, and Neva looked up at him to see if he was pulling her leg.

"No, seriously?" She asked. His cheeks burned dark pink from the laughter. "Seriously? What kinds of colors, like punk rock?"

"They've pretty much cornered the market on rainbow hair dye in these parts."

"Come sit by the fire!" The king's voice bellowed across the room, startling Neva, whose heart was already beating a little too fast from March's dark laughter and full mouth that quirked up into dimples at the corners.

The king waved to them. March pressed his hand against her lower back. "Come on, he won't stop until we do."

Not that sitting by the fire on a shoulder-high nest of pillows was really a trial. Neva settled herself on a yellow and orange cushion—after having to leap on to it on her belly, laughing along with the king and princess and all the giants nearby when they saw her performance. The fire was overly warm, causing her face to flush. She pushed her sleeves up. March clambered up on the purple cushion next to hers, after first divesting himself of his arrows and his bow. He smacked the cushion he sat on.

"Wine and song!" March unexpectedly proclaimed, looking around at the giants and flinging his arms out.

"You have been missed, my lord." The king laughed and motioned to someone Neva couldn't see. My lord? Indeed. Well, that explained the attitude problems. She eyed March. He could be a stand-in for Prince Charming, in one of the darker fairytales—without all the beheading and evisceration removed for the consumption of children. In his happiness, he looked not a day over twenty, maybe not even that, exuberant with his youth. He'd pulled his legs up under one another to sit Indian-style just like Neva had. She unwound her hair, sitting the scissors on her knee, and pulled her hair back again, twisting it into a knot. As she worked the scissors back into her hair, she glanced up to see March watching her with his mouth half-open, shock written all over his open face.

"What?" She smiled to cover her discomfort.

"You should wear your hair down." She rolled her eyes. Men always said that.

"Sure. And you should wear tighter pants." She raised an eyebrow in a mock leer.

He laughed in response, slapping his knee.

"So early, my lord?" The king's laughter peeled out of him, rich like strong coffee. "I am intrigued."

Neva looked up at his good-natured face, confused as to what he meant by his comment and unsure how to ask him to explain. He offered her a cup—a regular, human-sized cup that looked like a toy in his hand—and she accepted. She took a sip of whatever it was without hesitation, not having had a drink for some time. It was unfamiliar but sweet, almost cloying, like lychee or mango. From the corner of her eye, she saw March watching her, the smile gone from his face.

The king clapped his hands together and went off again with the princess in tow. When Neva balanced the cup on her knee, she noticed the embossing was of an apple tree with a snake dangling from a branch. That discomfited her.

"Whatever he asks you to do, you must do it. Anything. And please remember that they live here and feast continually through the year, and they always entertain themselves the same way, so they go to great lengths to find new things to entertain each other." The humor had bled out of him, and his earnest, fervent admonition scared her. This was another one of those "jump to the next level but only if you find the bunny under the bush" things.

"Is that all you can tell me?" She asked because it was only logical to at least ask if he could tell me more.

He sighed and smiled slightly. "Time works differently here, so I doubt they're up on current pop culture." He winked.

She rolled her eyes. People who winked all the time were usually either hiding something or trying to seem cute. She sipped her drink again. Now it tasted like pears and honey and allspice.

"Don't get too drunk, you'll screw everything up." March was really a big asshole sometimes. Neva glared at him.

"What? I've had two sips!" She took a huge gulp to punctuate that.

"It sneaks up on you. Like coconut rum." He looked down into his own cup, making an unreadable face. She guessed there was a story there. She didn't feel one iota of sympathy.

"Boo hoo, poor Prince Charming had a bad hangover. I cry for you." She took another drink and found her cup empty. Swinging her head around, *whoops!*, she sort of collapsed on her side on her pillow, laughing at herself as she did.

"Great," March grumbled. "I knew not to get my hopes up; smart independent types always have to make a point of standing up to me."

Neva once again had no idea what he was talking about. She sat up, about to ask him to explain himself, when Olwen popped back up. "Time for the celebrations to begin!"

A red-headed giantess in a magenta kimono-style dress, stood up from one of the tables as the king carried a chair over and plopped it down next to Neva's pillow. Apparently they didn't stand on ceremony. Olwen sat on several pillows on her father's other side. Right on the floor. Neva liked the giants more and more. But she needed another drink.

The giantess in the middle of the floor began speaking. "I knew a woman, lovely in her bones, when small birds sighed, she would sigh back at them, ah, when she moved, she moved more ways than one, the shapes a bright container can contain!"

"Theodore Roethke?" Neva whispered to March. He shrugged.

"Oh, you're knowledgeable about poetry?" The king peered down at her from over the arm of her chair. She must have spoken louder than she'd intended.

"I dated a guy who thought *he* was." She answered without thinking about it. March snorted, the king just grinned wider.

"Indeed, then you must recite us something." He waved, indicating—something. Neva figured she was supposed to get up and share with the rest of the class. She glanced at March. His tight facial expression told her what she needed to know. This was the "anything" she had to do.

She couldn't remember any poems—and even if she could, they would be too old, if the giants knew Roethke. Glancing up at the king's smile, she figured she at least had to try. This was obviously what would get them on to the next step.

"Can I sit here, or do I need to go stand over there?" She was going to do what had to be done, even if she'd rather choke to death on a peach pit.

"You may remain sitting." He turned further in his seat. Olwen sprawled on her pillows to look at Neva under the king's chair. Lots of chair legs scraped on the floor as the giants readjusted themselves for their entertainment.

"Oh shit," Neva whispered.

She didn't know any poems! She cleared her throat. She did, however, have a scary knack for memorizing song lyrics. Some songs were sort of like poems. She glanced at March, whose face had gone snow white in what looked like terror, the three moles high on his left cheekbone standing out sharply in his pale face.

Oh, screw it.

She opened her mouth and began to recite the poetry of popular music. After the first verse, she accidentally lapsed into singing, the sweet quince drink having addled her brain further than she'd realized.

She sang with her eyes closed, pretending she was in her car in Mobile, driving to the grocery or across the Bay to see her mom. She even let the Alabama slip all the way into her voice, mimicking Lyle Lovett's long vowels and twisted, elided consonants. Neva sang about Texas and cowboys and rural misery. When she opened her eyes back, Olwen blinked at her with her mouth open, slow smile sliding onto her face.

The king laughed, startling Neva almost ass over tea kettle off her pillow.

"You are unique!" He declared. "It has been long since one brought something unheard to us. I would that you would sing more."

And so Neva sang more. "Everybody Here Wants You" by Jeff Buckley, followed by a Sesame Street counting song, and "Silent All These Years" by Tori Amos. After that, her voice was shredded, and the king relented with raucous laughter and a stomp of his foot. Dancing commenced then, but Neva stayed on her pillow, sipping a new drink and wondering what was going to happen now.

"You, my dear, are startling and strange." The king leaned his chin on his palm. "I would offer you a boon."

Neva bit her bottom lip. "You mean a gift?"

He smiled, the lines around his eyes deepened dramatically. "Yes, a gift. Anything of mine is yours to take."

She didn't hesitate, pulling the golden scissors out of her hair. "I would like a lock of your hair, please." She had her manners, and she remembered to say please even if the hair situation was probably the only reason she was even there.

"That I would have given you anyway." He slid out of his chair and knelt by her pillow, inclining his head so that she could snip off a lock of his hair. She reached out and pulled a strand taut, surprised at how soft the thick hairs were. She cut a piece as long as the span from the tip of her ring finger to the base of her palm. The king sat back on his knees, resting his palms flat on his thighs.

"I offered you anything in my possession. You could have asked for all of my lands and holdings down to the last kernel of corn eaten by the last chicken in my yard." He paused. "And yet all you ask for is a lock of hair. Why is that?" His eyes were an odd blue with gold flecks.

"Because the hair is what I need to unbind March and get home again." She had no idea why anyone would want more than that. What was the point of asking for something other than the hair? Neva knew the lessons of greed and avarice, knew that path led to bitterness—especially in fairytales, where greed was so often the cause of backlash and curses. Why bring that upon herself if she didn't have to?

The king watched her for several long seconds as she clutched the thick strand of his hair in her hand. Suddenly, he slapped his thighs and stood, saying "Well, then. Rare indeed."

"You didn't want anything for yourself?" March asked. Neva turned to look at him, as the king ambled away out of her line of sight. He tilted his head to the side and licked his bottom lip.

"It *is* for me, because then I can do the next task and get back home. As fun as this is, I'd rather be in Mobile."

She polished off her drink, watching him watch her over the brim of the cup.

After what seemed a year to Neva, the king reemerged with a dog at his heels. The dog looked like a slightly over-sized greyhound. But it was pure white, and when the light shone through his ears they appeared blood red. The dog gave a series of short barks, pranced on his back feet, and bounded over to Neva. He licked her face enthusiastically, then nipped at her hair in his exuberance.

"His affection for you only bears out my own assumptions about you, child." The king reached into his pocket and pulled out a small wooden box. He extended his hand to Neva with the box sitting in his palm. "For your selflessness, I give you this." She reached out and took the box. She dumped it upside down onto her palm to find a golden ring in the shape of a twining vine and several bell-shaped flowers.

"I couldn't, really . . ." She held her hand out, so ingrained by the rules of her own culture that she couldn't consider taking a gift she didn't think she deserved or needed.

The king held up his hand. "This is a gift given freely. It is an insult to me for you not to accept it."

Neva frowned. The ring was pretty; she slipped it onto her finger. It fit her perfectly. She studied it for a moment, wondering what sort of spell it cast on her. She realized she'd put it on her wedding finger. Finally she looked up at the king. "Thank you, really. I love it."

"For entertaining me and my people, I gift you with this beast." The dog leapt in the air, doing an odd little twist. The dog was clearly more than a little high strung and crazy—just like Neva herself.

Olwen capered up and tugged her father toward the dancing. He smiled once more and waved.

"Well, damn, you did better than I expected. He usually only gives the dog, and even then he's fickle about it." He was amused.

Neva turned towards him, squinting her eyes. "What in the hell do you mean usually? Because I'm assuming those comments are directly related to all the other weird ones you and the king keep making." She glared at him.

"His name's Magog, by the way." March gulped down his drink until it was empty. "Since you asked, I'll tell you. Do you remember when you met me in the pub in Cardiff?" The words pub and Cardiff rolled out of his mouth with the Welsh lilt. Neva supposed he had no reason to learn to say either of them without it.

"Yeah, obviously." She made a move-it-along motion with her hand.

"Do you remember interceding on my behalf?" His small smile made a fleeting appearance.

"You mean the pushy girl and the claiming to be your girlfriend? Yes. And?" Neva had a very bad feeling that some sort of finality was about to transpire.

"You initiated a curse. By claiming me, you set this all in motion." March made a shooting motion with his right hand.

"What? I had no idea! What do you mean claiming? There was no claiming?"

"Well, obviously the magic involved in the *geas,* a sort of magical curse, thought there was a whole lot of claiming, and that's all that matters. Oh, aside from the fact you did it of your own volition with no collusion or undue influence."

"Your face is undue influence!" Neva declared before her brain caught up with her mouth.

March fell back against his pillow laughing. "And here I thought you were totally immune!"

Neva scowled at him. He propped himself up on his elbow, leaning on his side. "So now you have a year and a day to complete all of the tasks set before you. If you complete them, then you're released and so am I, to live on in the human world again until someone else claims me, and I start all over again."

"A year?" Neva screeched. "Oh hell no!"

"Calm down, it's only a year for you. Besides, you're the one who freely chose to jump into the pond. If you'd refused, I'd have been stuck here for three times that, but you'd have been fine." He pointed at her to emphasize how she'd made her own bed.

"Whatever. Why should I believe anything you say?" The fact was she really had little choice whether to believe him or not at this point.

"Have I lied to you yet?" He sat back up all the way, face as red at Olwen's dress, apparently not pleased to be accused of deceit.

Neva figured she might as well directly ask. "Why does either of us have to do any of this."

March watched her, his eyes in shadow. "Because I am cursed thusly."

Which seemed fairly self-evident to Neva. "Thusly *how*? And why *me*?"

With an elaborate sigh, March gestured between them both vaguely. "I'm cursed to repeat the same series of events over and over until someone breaks the curse."

Neva wondered why she'd gotten not only the cliché story, but also the uncommunicative prince. "So I break the curse and we're both free."

March's laughter hit her right beneath her belly button. "If you break the curse neither of us will ever be free."

The dog leaped up on her pillow, imposing himself between March and Neva, growling. She laid a hand on his bristling back.

"Great. The dog's got it out for me. Why the hell did I help you?" March flopped back onto his back.

"What're you talking about? Isn't that what you have to do? As part of the curse?" The giants had been pretty surprised by their arrival, and March had said there was another, longer way, but still . . .

"No, usually I give the line about the hair, hang out with the elves betting on fairy races, then come back when you've got the two pieces of hair." He sighed.

"Why did you help me, then?" Neva snitted. Screw him; she didn't need his help.

"Stupidity, apparently."

"Yeah, I endorse that assumption." She collapsed back onto her pillow, the dog turned three times in a circle next to her, then flopped down with his head on her stomach.

"Your mama." March mumbled.

CHAPTER FIVE

WHEN NEVA WOKE, sunlight threw fractals of violet and carmine and saffron, and every other exotic color Neva had ever seen, around the hall of the giants. She hadn't noticed the evening before that the outer walls of the hall were really floor to ceiling stained glass windows, their patterns repeating the same sort of nonsensical patterns as the floor tiles. The dog lifted his head from her belly when she sat up.

March sat crouched on the floor, an unfamiliar piece of fruit in his hand and two packs by him.

"Where is everyone?" Neva reflexively stroked the dog's neck. He turned his face up and licked her cheek as she struggled to pull her head back out of his reach. They struggled like that—she pulling back, the dog surging forward—until she wrapped her arm around his middle and restrained him. He began to shake and bark with an oddly deep yodel. The dog barked, and Neva felt something odd, something nameless, but it felt a lot like sitting in a room full of her family, not thinking about work or fretting about the future. A lot like safety.

"The giants keep different cycles from you. They are wakeful for days and sleep for days in turn." March regarded her from the floor, perhaps ten feet in front of her and three feet below. He was being unreadable again, wide awake and eyes bored. She didn't really want to deal with him, having just woken up again with no coffee in sight. She was actually sort of surprised she wasn't going through caffeine withdrawal. By her count she'd been out of the human world at least twenty-four hours.

"So they're asleep." Neva said. March unwrapped himself from his crouch, brushing a hand through his hair as he did so. The dog watched him, with a fierce expression.

"Or somewhere else. I am known to them, but they are less known to me." He smiled, head tilted somewhat to the side, and Neva saw that he was making some kind of joke. The kind of joke she didn't get in the least.

"Whatever. What's with the bags?" She wanted a pot of coffee and a hot shower. And maybe some Krispy Kreme. Or a Hardee's biscuit. "I'm hungry."

March stooped back over, and the dog leapt to his feet, unsteady on the pillow. Neva held onto the skinny animal to keep him from sliding off; the light from the windows shone crimson through his ears. March pulled a piece of fruit from one of the bags and lobbed it at her under-handed, with no effort.

The fruit was peachy and pinkish, oblong, with one end sharper than the other, similar to a papaya. She bit down, and it tasted like a blueberry cake Krispy Kreme doughnut. She almost spat it out from shock.

March laughed at what her. "The more cynical your

kind become, the more amazed you become, simultaneously. It would be amusing if it wasn't mostly depressing."

"I guess it's pointless to ask 'what' or 'how' since the answer is magic, right? Or pointless even to pick up on the phrase 'your kind'?" She slid down the slope of the satin pillow to land softly on her feet. The dog leapt down to stand next to her. Neva patted her pocket for the lock of the Giant King's hair—Magog's hair—and munched on the doughnut fruit.

"It's easier to say yes. So I will. Yes, it's magic." He picked up one of the packs and slung it on. His quiver nested next to it and his bow stuck out of the top.

"We're on to the next stop?" Neva didn't quibble. She just grabbed the other pack and inspected it before putting it on. The backpack was square, like the packs soldiers wore in the First World War; a clicking lock mechanism formed what Neva thought at first was a silver Celtic knot that pulled apart like a magnetic clasp. When she looked closer at the knot she realized it was an intertwined nest of snakes. The straps and backpack itself were woven from some type of flexible cloth. It was black. Neva looked at March in his black on black on black ensemble. She thought maybe he liked to match.

The pack felt light. She suddenly remembered the hair in her pocket and shifted the pack onto one shoulder to open it and deposit her goodies. Her shawl and all of her extra clothes were in the pack.

"You went through my panties?" Neva looked up at him blinking with a falsely scandalized face.

March could go from totally opaque to startlingly transparent. Just then, he was shocked. Neva looked at him. He took a step toward her, and the dog paced around and sat right on her feet, staring up at March with a half-snarl on his snout.

"I . . . was trying to be helpful." He stammered.

Neva ignored him, and clicked the knot of snakes back together, and flipped the pack back onto her back.

"Let's ride," she said.

"I wish." March smirked slightly, his awkwardness fluttering off him like lint. "Procuring mounts would be tedious, to say the least."

Neva watched the light on March's face drift from jade to cobalt as he stepped around her and toward the rotunda leading to the outside. The colors made crisp impressions on his pale cheek.

"It's an expression," she replied, even though she knew he knew.

"So is 'like, duh'." He was ahead of her, so she couldn't see his face, but she thought he was probably laughing.

Neva followed March through the riotous rotunda and out through the front of the giant's mansion. When they stepped onto what Neva remembered as a path through the lawn, she had a moment's vertigo because ahead of her there was no such path. Instead there was a garden of towering hydrangea bushes shuddering and waving on stalks as thick as Neva's leg. The clusters of flowers were at least three feet across. A heather-purple and violet bloom gave up the ghost and drifted down to land on the knot in Neva's hair. When she reached back and pulled it away, it was the size of her hand. She rubbed it against her cheek, the petals warming to her skin and feeling like baby-soft flesh moving against her face. Her eyes drifted closed, and she smiled without thinking.

When she opened her eyes, March stood staring with

his eyebrow raised. "You are a strange creature." There was a smile in his tone.

Behind him, disappearing into the hydrangea bushes, was a flag-stone path.

"The yellow-brick road?" She dropped the flower and nodded towards him.

"Something like that." He turned and started walking. She followed him, with the dog leaping onto his back legs and barking happily with his entire body bent back on itself.

Neva laughed, watching the dog, smelling the green scent of dirt and chlorophyll and open sky, all familiar but somehow crisper, with no undertone of car exhaust or clinging humidity. The path wound in a serpentine pattern so that she could only see a few feet ahead at a time.

"Is something going to jump out on me?" She gripped her pack and looked from one side of the path to the other.

"What kind of something?" March's voice tripped off his tongue jagged with laughter.

"Heffalump?" Neva smiled.

March cocked his head and squinted his eyes. "Did you make that up?" The dog skittered on the stones of the path and leaped between Neva and March, growling low in his throat and his hackles coming up. "Oh, shut up, you idiot!"

Neva reached down and stroked the dog's translucent ears. "Hey, you shut up."

March rolled his ears. "What are you going to name it?" He flicked his head towards the dog.

Neva looked down at the hound, who was almost wrapped around her leg, and over at March who was studiously not looking at the dog.

"Do you not like dogs or something?" To her, that was paramount to baby-eating, but she'd known a few people with real phobias: people who had been bitten as children or seen other people mauled. But where Neva came from, there was no discussion of "dog people" or "cat people". Everyone either owned a dog or tolerated them—it was a fact of life so ingrained it was never questioned. Neva's granddaddy raised blueticks and black and tans for hunting, and her mother had a pack of Yorkies and corgies. She was the only member of her family currently with no dog, and that was only due to the fact that her twelve-year-old Australian shepherd had died the year before and she hadn't had the heart to buy a puppy yet.

March just stared down at the dog. "No, dogs are . . ." He paused. "Dogs just are. This one appears to not like me much."

He was right about that. However, Neva suspected there was a whole lot more going on with that than she had a clue about, just like how everything else with March seemed to be only half exposed.

"What are you going to call it?" March asked again, stepping to the side slightly. The dog backed off of Neva's leg a little, moving to walk in an actual line, relaxing now that March was further away.

He said "call it" not "name it". And Neva thought about that for a second. Why would he choose his words so carefully? Because he obviously did, able to slide fluidly from Welsh vernacular to current American slang. His language proficiency must be magical or a super power or something.

"What would you call him?" The hydrangeas stopped abruptly—a razor-blade line of stalks ending a few feet from a Roman-style aqueduct that stretched away along the horizon.

"By his name," March said after a long pause. "How you knew to ask that . . ." He broke off, looking down at her with open assessment.

"By a logical path, March. Not that I'd expect you to grasp that, coming from a place with no rhyme or reason."

"We have lots of rhyme, actually." The smirk bled into his words.

"Har har." She looked up at him, his hair flying around his face in the tiny eddies of breeze that blew out of the hydrangea forest, his cheeks bright red against the black of his clothes. "What's his name?"

March turned his face away from her and took a half step forward. "Cafal."

The dog's ears pricked up at his name, and he turned his head in an odd quirk, watching March's back.

"Cafal?" Neva asked the dog, who snapped his head up at her voice and stood. "Okay, I guess so. Let's hit it, Cafal."

His head moved into her hand as she opened it palm down towards him.

March was easy to follow in the open ground beyond the aqueduct, a black figure in a landscape of low-growing green on green. The path still meandered, but with nothing to obstruct the view Neva could see it far in the distance. She surveyed the new vista, turning around in a tight circle to take in the aqueduct behind them and the hydrangeas shuddering against each other beyond that. She was kind of surprised that the bushes and aqueduct hadn't just disappeared, blipped right out of existence, leaving nothing but the new landscape all the way from horizon to horizon.

As she looked more closely, she saw that dividing the green were tiny rivulets of blue. The field was actually a webbed swampland. She wondered about the stability of the path. She watched March ahead of her, his step steady, shoulders rolling with his walk. They walked like that for some time. There was no way to gauge how long, since the sun overhead always maintained its zenith.

They walked like that, Neva listening to the faint sounds of water running and Cafal's nails on the stone, of wind rustling against the swamp scrub and the sounds of her own clothing brushing against itself. She didn't feel tired particularly, even though she rarely exerted herself that much, and she didn't have to pee or feel any need to drink.

And all of those bodily function issues were strange. Really weird in a way that she couldn't really think about anything else. Why would she suddenly feel like she could walk forever with no food or water or need to relieve herself? Cafal never broke from the path to scamper into the swamp to drink or lift his leg. March, well, she wasn't so surprised by him, because he was obviously not exactly human, or if human then one who had been altered by long exposure to magic.

Then it occurred to her that she was thinking of magic as an empirically quantifiable factor that could and would have an impact upon a person. She'd never been a huge skeptic—she left the door open to the possibility that aliens could be real, and being Southern, the existence of ghosts seemed self-evident in the odd creepiness of rotting plaster and mildew stains of old homes. But she'd never believed in mystical wackiness, never experimented with ouija boards or chanted Bloody Mary in mirrors as a kid. Thinking of magic as something like the laws of physics was also something new, something odd for her to think.

She was lost in thought like that for some time, trying to work out if magic could affect a person like repeated exposure to X-rays or ingestion of lead paint. Could magic build up in a person, like radiation, and eventually change the very nature of who someone was? Or could it bleed into someone's organs and sit there, waiting to leach out into a person's system, manifesting like poison, in hair going naturally pink or footsteps leaving sprouting daisies? She took a deep breath and exhaled all of her thoughts with it. The air smelled like the ocean.

March had stopped up ahead of her. She hurried to catch up to him. When she did, she could see to the right that all the streamlets converged in the middle distance into a wide, lazy river so far across she couldn't see the opposite bank. The path jagged sharply to the left and down, becoming a series of wide, shallow steps in soil becoming less lush, sandy.

"Are we at the beach?" Cafal sat next to her, pressing his body into her leg.

March descended the first step, looking at her over her shoulder. "Why would you guess that and not the desert?" He only sounded interested, not sarcastic.

"I can smell the salt in the air, and that river's forming a delta." She pointed at it, snaking away in tentacles all along the flat plateau to the right.

March's eyes stared back at her foam green and turquoise. "Do you feel an affinity for the ocean?" He cocked his head, his eyelashes brushing his cheek when he looked down at Cafal.

"I suppose." She'd lived on the coast her whole life. Affinity wasn't really a word she'd use to describe that, but perhaps . . .

"Hm," March said, moving down to the next stair. "We'll see, I guess. Should be fun!" He threw his head back laughing, bright and joyous and vital.

His exuberance worried her somewhat. He seemed like

the type to take quite a bit of pleasure out of other people's pain and anguish, or maybe she was just being mean to think that. She frowned at his back but followed.

In the way of this place the stairs from the top had seemed to sit right on top of soft, sandy soil, but when she stepped down onto them, in a rush of vertigo, she was on a set of wooden stairs leading down a steep sand dune. The stairs followed the slope of the white dune. The wood looked rickety and ancient, dark like it had been under the tideline for years and resurrected. There was no railing, just the waist-high sand. She reached out and ran her fingers through it, bringing the tips up to her face to look at the grains. They were colorless, the sunlight fractured where it hit the small particles. It was quartz sand, only white when heaped up on itself, the same as the fur on a polar bear.

The stairs descended down, down, down, for a measureless amount of time. Suddenly, over March's shoulders, Neva could see the ocean, an undulating shimmer of ultramarine and teal and green rippling with small waves. No white caps. No steep cliffs. The water rolled up to the shore gently without foam or urgency. The beach lay against the water just as white as the dunes they'd walked through.

Neva felt like shoving March out of the way and rushing down to the beach, but he kept up a steady pace, and she tamped down the desire. Cafal nipped at her sleeve and barked once, his tail wagging so hard that when it slapped her leg it stung even through her pants.

March looked back over his shoulder, his blank expression turning his features sharp—Neva was beginning to suspect that the blank look was something he'd developed over a long time, not natural to him. "What?" he said.

"What do you mean 'what'?" she snapped, feeling

somewhat undone. There was an urgency to do something that she could vaguely taste on the back of her tongue but couldn't name.

"What is wrong with you?" His tone, a combination of concerned and angry, betrayed the blank face.

"Nothing." It was such a lie that the second syllable faded at her lips, not getting anywhere near a real airing.

Then she did shove him out of the way and ran down the steps, the backpack bouncing with her movements, Cafal barking and bounding next to her. She felt March reach out to grab her, his fingers snatching on the knot on the pack, but just as he did, her foot hit the sand and the deserted beach sprang into life.

As her foot hit what she expected to be yielding sand, Neva instead stepped off the wooden stairs onto wet cobblestones. She stood on the edge of a wide arcade paved with interlocking sepia stones shaped like octagons. To her left the sea lapped up onto the stones, rocking back and forth in aquamarine, beyond the shoreline buildings rose up, their foundations under the water, some with doorways leading into open air. Far out, down the flooded street she could see winding out, it broke the surface with a splash. The buildings jutted at weird angles, one story often appearing not to sit evenly on the one below it, like a straw stuck into a glass looks bent above and beneath the surface of a drink.

She turned in a circle. On the other three sides of the arcade buildings clustered together, damp and shining in the sun, little alleys and streets pushed their façades apart, allowing Neva to see further into the clean, salt-stained city. All the buildings had waterlines clearly marked.

"This is . . . surprising." March said from behind her, his voice twisted into his version of ironic.

Neva turned to look at him, bright sunlight showing

blue highlights in his black hair, shock eroding his careful facial expression.

"Where are we?" She would have added, 'what the hell's going on?' but knew that was pointless.

"A place with many names." His voice trailed off, or Neva thought it did, because she noticed the tide was going out, exposing more and more of the submerged part of the city, in an unnaturally swift manner. She watched as more and more buildings were revealed—spires with impossibly fluttering banners far in the distance, salmon colored cathedral in the middle distance, fairytale cottages and gingerbread-looking houses abutting the arcade.

The water retreated and retreated until the only hint left of the ocean was the smell of the sea and the dampness clinging to the stones.

Neva drew a breath to ask March a series of what were sure to be useless questions when Cafal let out a yip and sat on Neva's foot. She shifted her pack on her shoulders and swung her head in the direction the dog was looking.

Suddenly, like a television clearing from static snow to perfect clarity, the arcade shuddered to life, people appeared around her, stalls and carts and animals and produce blipped into existence, the accompanying smells and noise flooding in two seconds later. March and Neva now stood next to a wooden stall heaped high with fifteen different varieties of seaweed, from long pieces of brown kelp to desiccated bunches of sargassum with tiny berry-like buds trembling in the eddies of air produced by the seaweed-monger's bustling. The people were dressed in something Neva would describe as Hollywood fairytale, smocks and skirts and wooden shoes on the women, men in straight-legged pants and white shirts and hats.

"Nori?" The seaweed hawker was a middle-aged man,

thin with reddish blond hair sticking up on the top of his head in a crest like a cockatoo.

Neva snapped her mouth closed, her teeth clicking together. "I . . . I . . . don't like nori."

"Not even teriyaki nori?" The man looked surprised, as though Neva had just stripped naked and painted herself with peanut butter.

"Come on," March grabbed her by the elbow, kicking at Cafal when he growled softly, getting a snarl in return.

"Let go of me," Neva snatched her arm away, bumping into March because the movement caused her to lose balance. He steadied her with a hand wrapped around her back and braced on her hip, bringing her flush to his side. He smelled like leather and apples and sunshine. His hand spanned the entire space from her waist to the top of her thigh, steady and firm without hurting her.

They passed a stall selling jewelry made from pearls and coral and mother of pearl, then one selling fishing hooks made from what looked like ivory—or more likely scrimshaw. March took his hand off her hip, and he trailed the backs of his fingers up her spine to the nape of her neck. It made her shiver. She pulled away, elbowing him in the side, and squinting up at him.

He was smiling, dimples deep in his cheeks, face flushed with amusement. "Your hair's coming undone."

"Right." She reached behind her, pulled the scissors out of her hair, stuck them between her teeth by the finger loops, and unknotted then reknotted her hair. She wanted to wash it, brush it out, take a shower. As she stuck the scissors back into her hair, she nodded her chin at a stall selling squid and shellfish. "Do you notice a theme around here?"

"They live off the sea." March said, light, the edge of laughter tracing his words.

"No, really?" Neva rolled her eyes. "What is this place?"

"The Drowned City, Ys, Lyonesse, it has many names." March looked over her head at something. Lyonesse sounded vaguely familiar, but she couldn't place where from, probably some Led Zepplin song or something. "I should have known this would happen." He sighed, long and rough and slightly broken.

Neva turned from puzzling out the gelatinous matter one of the venders was hawking to look up with him, then followed his line of sight to the sky beginning to curve and bow into evening. Camellia pink streamers skidded across the sky—or what Neva could see of it with the tarps over the various stalls obscuring her sight. March's jaw clenched and unclenched when she looked at his profile, obviously gritting his teeth.

Grabbing him by the sleeve, Neva yanked him along her, winding among people dressed in greens and blues and grays, all with disheveled hair that curled against their necks and faces in wet tendrils. They passed fishmongers and net-menders, artists purveying anything and everything covered in shells, an open-air barbeque pit sizzling with shrimp on skewers, boatswains, and a sandalmaker. Finally, the avenue of stalls ended at an alley between two one-story buildings that wept salt water from their wooden shingles, tracks of salt running down their facades in crystalline rambles. Neva tugged March into the alley with Cafal bounding and cavorting at their heels.

Digging her fingers into March's arm, Neva whirled around and squinted up at him, making eye contact. He smirked down at her, reaching up to push his hair out of his face with his free hand. "What happens during this part of the quest?" Asking him directly seemed to have worked every other time, so she was going to stick with that.

"This isn't part of the quest, thus my whole remark about being surprised a while ago." He lifted one eyebrow and made what Neva assumed was his wry face.

"What do you mean?" Her heart sped up and her pulse began beating in her wrists and neck so hard she could feel it. His face dipped closer to hers as he shifted his weight slightly, moving the pack on his back. One of his eyebrows quirked up at the far corner and the other quirked down by his nose. His eyes dilated slightly and his mouth parted just enough to allow him to suck in a breath.

He stared down at her, and she tightened her hand further, grasping hard enough to bruise, hard enough she felt the bones of her fingers bruising him.

"I thought this might be happening, when the sand appeared, but I've never come so far on this trip, so I wasn't sure." Making no move to pull away from her or wincing at how hard Neva held him, he reached up and pushed a piece of hair behind her ear. "I thought . . ." He paused, blinking slowly, face brightening to a soft rose. "Because you're strong, and you're from their realm, you might call them."

Neva, while really not wanting to, actually sort of understood what he was saying. "You mean because I grew up by the ocean I made this happen?"

March shrugged slightly. "Maybe. People don't cross over much any more, and she'd want to see one of her own."

"Who the hell is *she*? And why are you acting so weird. Do you not like the sea? Does it hurt you? Is this bad? I mean, does this screw up the whole quest? Will you be stuck here forever, or will I get trapped here? Or, you know, will I be stuck here for a year and not get to hurry up . . ." Trailing off, she tried to think of any other questions she could cram in, any other bases she could cover, worried that she was forgetting some important angle that would end up screwing her over.

"Could you . . ." March peeled her fingers off his arm. She hadn't even remembered she was holding him. He pulled back his sleeve to rub at the fingerprint bruises. Neva watched the muscles in his forearm slide and slip against each other under his skin. "I'm not worried about you, Neva."

She snapped her eyes back to his. He never said her name.

"I'm selfishly worried about myself." He smiled, lips red enough to look lipsticked, eyes falling closed, and the look was a cross between beatific and pained.

"Dahut does not like to be turned down." The voice came from the mouth of the alley. Neva spun around, smacking March with her pack. He grunted as Cafal began barking.

Three men stood in the breach between the first two tumble-down houses. They were dressed like rejects from a minstrel show—tights and clown-shoes and crushed velvet tunics and floppy velvet hats, each in a primary color, one blue, one orange, and one green. Each man was beautiful in his own way—one with burnt sugar freckles and eyes as big and blue as the mid-day sky; one with sandy blond hair hanging to his chin and a jaw square enough to use as a level; one with cinnamon skin and grey eyes.

"My lady," the blond in green bowed, doffing his silly hat. "Our Grace would like to offer you her hospitality."

The black man in blue made some sort of complex

greeting towards March. "My Lord, you do us great honor."

March made a grumbly, annoyed noise behind Neva's back. "Whatever."

The freckled man in orange made the same motions that the green-clad man had. "Our Grace would request the honor of your voice, my Lord."

Neva twisted her head around to blink at March. "You have some kind of magic thing you do with your voice?"

March lifted an eyebrow. "And here I thought you were smart for one of your kind. Where's the logic? She wants me to sing."

The idea of March singing sent so much blood to Neva's face that she went slightly light-headed. March's raised eyebrow gained a twin. "Do you have a request?" he whispered, bumping against her back and chuckling softly.

Neva's blush faded with her annoyance at the spark of shame she felt at his flirting.

"We will accompany you to the palace," Blue guy said, even though no one had agreed to go. Neva imagined the invitation wasn't really optional.

"Whatever." Neva echoed March's remark, and probably his opinion on this diversion from their journey.

The minstrels led them out of the jumble of the market area into a more formal mercantile district. Clothing shops and musical instrument makers and stores Neva couldn't really comprehend sat neatly and harmoniously next to one another in a slithering pattern that could be called a street, but would probably be more accurately termed a pig path. The cobbled streets wound in such a way that one couldn't see further than the s-bend one was traversing at the time.

When they left the business district they wandered onto an actual boulevard, straight and wide and lined with trees so thick and closely packed that Neva couldn't see the buildings behind them. The branches of the trees seemed to lock together from one tree to the next, twining together to form a wall of solid green. The trunks were thick like oaks, but the branches liquid and dripping like willows.

The wide boulevard bled into a water garden consisting of linked ponds topped by jets that fountained high into the air and skipped from pond to pond. Hibiscus and mimosa bushes shook in the spray from the jets, orange and pink and red blooms livid in the dark foliage. Beyond the water garden rose a palace of pink coral and abalone shell, insubstantial in the growing dusk. The sky seemed to sit right on the building, the clouds morphing into a roof. When they passed one of the ponds, the rose of the sky and pink of the building reflected in the momentarily still water so that Neva couldn't make out where sky left off and the building began.

March wrapped his arm around Neva's back, pulling her nearer to him with his hand on her hip. She gazed up at him, enraptured by the shining opalescence of the mother of pearl inlay of the pillars running across the front of the palace, twinkling even from a distance in low light.

His expression was his blank one, the one that was meant to give nothing away but that Neva knew masked concern or anger. "When we get inside, don't freak out."

And if there was ever a sentence that induced the exact opposite reaction to that which was intended, it was that one. "What do you mean, 'freak out'? What's going to happen? Ultra-violence? More curses? Will I be forced to eat pig entrails?"

March smiled slightly. "You're completely insane, which is a plus. Nothing's going to happen to you, chill."

Which meant that something was going to happen to him or she was going to have to do something. She didn't particularly like either option.

"Did you sleep with someone's wife?" His hand was still lodged firmly on her hip, and she wasn't moving away, but she was considering it.

"Oddly enough, quite the opposite." The smile in his voice almost distracted her from the fantastic mosaic they were walking over—a ten foot octopus so life-like it almost seemed to be waving its arms.

The three minstrel pageboys walked up the long, low, wide steps that ran the length of the façade of the palace. Neva and March followed, March dropping his hand from Neva's hip. When they crested the stairs and Neva could see between the abalone-encrusted pillars, her mouth dropped open. The "palace" was really just a long open-air gallery framing a vast, mosaic inlaid floor stretching out right into the ocean. The tiles were blue and grey and aqua in a rippling pattern that mimicked the sea lapping at the edges of the octagonal expanse.

There appeared to be quite a shindig happening on what, upon stepping on it, Neva discovered was a pontoon. The water wasn't just coming up to the edges—the whole thing was built right on the sea. It rocked slightly, just enough to be noticeable but not enough to pitch her off her feet.

Like the three men who'd brought them there, all the people at the party were wearing primary colors in stereotypical medieval tunics and high-bodiced dresses. On the left-hand side of the shimmering floor was a series of octagonal tables of various sizes aligned like some sort of undulating sea monster's vertebrae. On the tables sat fragile-looking glasses in red and blue and yellow and green with long, curving stems and flutes shaped like up-turned jellyfish and plates of the same bright glass brimming with pink and cream squid tentacles and shining silver fish and jewel-like sushi rolls and glistening caviar. The people fluttered across the floor in spinning steps that may have been dancing or may have been a naturally fluid dexterity. Like the people in the market, all of their hair curled wildly, damp as though they'd just come from the bath, leaving dark patches on their shoulders and various places their hair touched their flowing clothes.

At the far end of the pontoon sat several chairs constructed from shells, some occupied some not. On the right side of the pontoon a lively band played a tune on harps and violins and pipe instruments. March sighed loudly, and Neva turned in his direction to see a woman with golden-red hair so long and thick it almost seemed alive and writhing approaching them. She was barefoot and wearing green. Holding her hair away from her face was a tiara of rainbow pearls—pink and white and grey in the glowing copper of her long hair.

March sighed again, slouching slightly so that his shoulder was level with the top of Neva's head. He ran his hand through his hair and scratched his cheek; both moves intended to cover extreme agitation, Neva figured. The threat apparently was this sashaying bundle of silk and pearls. When she came close enough, Neva saw that she was beautiful, but that was only to be expected. Slightly up-turned nose and full mouth, round cheeks and green eyes streaked with gold.

"You surprise me, my Lord," the woman's voice fell from her mouth like the proverbial bells chiming.

"You brought me here, Dahut," March said, voice tight. Neva looked up at him, trying to read his expression but only able to see his profile. The minstrels had called her 'Our Grace', and she addressed March with an honorific, but he did not return the formality. That had to mean something.

Dahut tilted her head from side to side, her hair fluttering. She unnerved Neva for no reason she could name. "I brought one of Llyr's own, not you, my Lord."

Neva was confused and a little scared. Something really wrong was going on. And she couldn't just ask March, because Dahut seemed to be a real threat. Who was Llyr? Was March really Prince Charming, like, for real? "That is of no consequence." He sounded tired, defeated even. Neva knew that something beyond her understanding was happening here—had been happening ever since she'd jumped into the pond—but this felt different, wrong somehow.

"You came willingly, of your own volition, knowing I would claim you." Dahut smiled, the smile appearing bright like sunshine off of water. The hair on the back of Neva's arms stood on end.

Claim? That didn't sound good.

March made a sound between a moan and a scoff.

"What do you mean claim?" Neva asked, reaching back to fiddle with her hair. Dahut turned her attention from March to Neva.

"I would have him as my lover." Her smile returned, brighter still. "I do not like being denied that which I covet."

March met her eyes when Neva looked up at him. "Um, this is a long story?"

He rolled his eyes. Neva took that as a yes.

"Do you want to . . . you know?" Neva more mouthed than whispered. In her regular life, Neva would never ask someone if they wanted to sleep with someone else on such short acquaintance—but as events proved, this was not in any way her regular life.

He blinked at her slowly, with disdain.

"He has resisted me." The darkness in Dahut's tone wasn't alleviated by her perfect voice.

Neva watched March's jaw clench. She had no idea why any man would resist this woman, but March had been reluctant with the nubile young girls in Cardiff as well. He was strange. Or possibly gay. Neva looked up at his ruler-straight cheekbone and the tight line of his jaw, at the black lashes long enough to look fake, his black hair curling against his ear and cheek. Definitely gay.

"Well, too bad. He's with me." Neva figured the whole "he's my boyfriend" thing had gotten her into this, so maybe repeating it would get her out of it. She crossed her fingers behind her back and held her breath.

March let out a bark of laughter, tossing his head back and clapping his hands together with a loud smack. Dahut looked startled, or as close to startled as someone with no real facial expression could.

"You belong to my Lord." Dahut said, somewhere between a question and a statement, her head cocking back and forth like a bird.

"Um . . ." Neva squinted, trying to puzzle that out. By my Lord did she mean March—who she'd called that—or someone else? "Maybe?" She wasn't up on the rules and regs here still, so she had no idea if, maybe technically, she did sort of maybe kind of belong to March—like Cafal belonged to her in the same way. She had just compared herself to a dog. Great.

"You do not take precedence over my Lord." Dahut spat at March with an overwrought line-reading reminiscent of a badly-made gothic romance.

"I have made no claim on her, only her on me." March

smiled like a lunatic and wiped a tear of laughter from below one eye with his thumb before wrapping his arm around Neva's shoulders and rocking her back and forth against his side. He leaned down and kissed the top of her head.

She figured she'd just walked into something else stupid.

Dahut picked up her skirt with one long, white, be-pearled hand and strolled away. March twisted around so that he faced Neva, his arm still around her back. He leaned down and pressed his lips right against the curve of her ear.

"You really pissed her off. I love you a little for that." He breathed out in short bursts of laughter, and blood rushed to Neva's face and her stomach muscles tightened.

The pages reappeared, all looking dour and surly. "You are our honored guest, my lady."

March stepped back but kept his hand resting on Neva's knapsack. She noticed the pages were now being pointedly rude to March, which she didn't totally mind. He didn't seem to care, from the dimpled grin on his face and the insouciant wink he shot the page in blue.

"That's great. When do I get to leave?" Neva sometimes had trouble being subtle.

The pages didn't take offence, however. They just began bustling around her, upsetting Cafal who growled and snipped, and swarming so that she and March were forced to walk to a set of shell chairs next to a low table.

"When we all do, my lady," the page in yellow informed her.

"What does that mean?" Neva asked March, whose hand had slid up to the back of her neck, twisting a piece of her hair around his finger.

"We have to spend the night here. No one leaves Ys at night. It's part of the enchantment. That's why I was so annoyed at the sunset. However," he tugged at her hair almost hard enough to hurt. "Now, I'm not annoyed!" He punctuated that with a couple more tugs on her hair and a rumbling chuckle.

The pages attempted to divest Neva of her knapsack, and Cafal took great umbrage, latching onto the ankle of the page in orange and setting off a chain reaction of buffoonery in which the men alternated between being harassed by the dog and attempting to "help" Neva become more comfortable.

When she was finally settled, and all three pages were wincing in their now tattered clothes, the orange page made some sort of obeisance with his hand to his forehead. "If there is anything, anything, we can do to make your visit more pleasant, I beg you to ask."

With that, all three made the forehead gesture again, and they walked away with as much dignity as men in silly costumes could. Neva sagged in her seat and watched March steadily consuming a large plate of calamari.

"Well, that was effusive as hell." She was tired suddenly and desperately wanted a shower or a bath and to change her clothes.

"They just want to get you away from me so that Dahut can try to grope me." He licked his fingers and waggled his eyebrows. Neva smiled back at him despite her best efforts not to.

"What's her problem anyway? Some kind of brain-damaged succubus or something?" Neva picked up a plate of oysters and, finding no fork, plucked the muscle out of the shell with her fingers, then tipped her head back and plopped it in her mouth. She looked up to find March watching her with his changeable eyes more green than blue. "What? There are no forks. What's up with Dahut?"

He sighed. "You know, the usual: cursed princess. She also happens to be a voracious man-eater who was cursed because she swore herself to the wrong man and then slept her way through her kingdom."

"So this is the fairy tale about the oppression of women's sexuality?" Neva wondered if the "man eater" appellation was literal. She ate two more oysters waiting for March's reply.

"She sleeps with whomever she wants, whether or not the man's compliant." He sat back in his chair. "Is it oppression if she's a rapist?"

He had a point there. "Did she do that to you, is that the big drama between you?"

March shook his head slightly. "If she had, she wouldn't be so interested. She tried, but I evaded her last time."

"Is she the one who cursed you?" It would fit, Neva thought.

March's smile was his secret one. He sighed, long and low, shhhhh, through his teeth. "You ask so many questions that eventually you'll ask them all and find the right one."

"So that's a no, then." Neva spat out a piece of oyster shell into her hand and then deposited it onto her plate. "If I leave you alone she'll just come jump on you even though I done laid my claim on you?" She had put on a silly, fake southern accent for the last little bit.

"I'm pretty positive that if she isn't convinced we're a couple, she'll bind me to her for the night, whether you're sitting right here or not." He looked defeated again. Neva could see no reason for a man to turn down a woman like Dahut unless he had some serious psychological issues or was only interested in other men. She reached across the table and wedged a couple fingers into March's open fist and squeezed.

"Are you holding my hand?" He asked with a small laugh.

"If she poisons me, I'll be pissed at you." She winked.

Neva was just about to ask *why* he didn't want to sleep with Dahut when he lifted their hands, twisting hers up so that the palm was exposed, then leaned down and licked the place on her palm where the oyster shell had rested. His tongue was scandalously pink and sharp against the lines of her hand. His eyes never left hers. When she sucked in a breath to insult him, his face blushed hard and his pupils blew wide, leaving only a thin rim of color.

So, maybe not gay.

CHAPTER SIX

WHEN NEVA LOOKED up from March's eyes, she gasped in shock. The room spun around her, the edges blurring and whipping in a frenzy. Her stomach dropped to her feet and her eyes wouldn't focus. When her vision adjusted and the topsy-turvy feeling of falling stopped, the sea and tiled pontoon were gone. Shifting lights flickered around a cavernous room. White light floated over March's face and over the floor and walls when she twisted her head around. Instead of an open-air pavilion they were seated in what appeared to be a room of sea-green glass. The light rippled over them like sun through ice in a steady rocking motion.

"Oh my god." Neva, despite everything that had happened to her already, was flabbergasted—talking animals and giants whatever, blinking your eyes and teleporting or into a totally different place was just weird, and com-

pletely vertigo-inducing. The entire party had been trans-
ported in the blink of an eye.

"The sun has set all the way," March rubbed his thumb
over the place on her palm where he had licked.

"Okay, and?" Neva knew there was a huge workboot
still to drop.

"The city's underwater now." His face was tight, up-
tilted eyes wrinkling at the corners in either anger or agitation, mouth dimpling at the edges.

"Is this bad?" She wished she knew which sort of direct question to ask. But she couldn't quite bring herself
to ask if the courtiers were about to bust out the knives
and fangs.

"Maybe. It depends on a lot of things." He turned his
head, looking over his shoulder towards a clutch of twit-
tering and giggling, brightly dressed folks. "Depends
maybe on one thing."

"What thing?" Not that Neva really expected to understand what he said anyway. He liked to speak in confus-
ing aphorisms.

"Who's in charge." He stood and picked up his bow,
quiver and pack. He looked down at her, his bangs falling
in his eyes. "You want a bath? I think we can hook that
up." His smile emerged lopsided and knowing in a way
someone his age shouldn't have been able to manage.

"Yeah, sure, whatever." She didn't argue the change of
subject, not with so many people around. As she shrugged
her knapsack back on, she wondered when she'd started
trusting March. The truth was, he might be more dangerous than any of these vapid people.

She followed him, watching the glass beneath her feet
as she did. The strobing light roiled under the translucent material, turning the surface yellow in places, ab-
sence of light turning it almost blue in others. The glass

had a slight texture, striations that she supposed were to keep the courtiers from slipping and busting their heads open. If they could break their heads open. Who knew if they were human or possessed some ability to keep themselves erect on slick surfaces she didn't. The walls and ceiling melted together so that the room was shaped like a cave.

Beyond the ballroom, the hall spread out between pillars of glass. The colors altered slightly, becoming clearer, almost completely transparent. Instead of opening into a vast span of glass floor like Neva expected, the pillars appeared to be the edges of doorways. March walked past several, and Neva looked through the gaps down corridors of blue and green and yellow glass. March stopped and looked over his shoulder at her.

"Why isn't anyone stopping us from wandering around?" That was only one of about a hundred questions she had.

"They don't care what we do. They don't care about much." His tone was definitely derisive. Huh. So March was definitely not a fan of any of the people here, not just Dahut.

"You want to tell me what your issue is?" She poked him in the back when he turned down one of the corridors. "And how you know your way around?" She knew the answer to the second one; that was obvious—he had been there before.

"I don't like enclosed spaces." And that was all he apparently had to say about that. Neva watched the light through the walls. It was really amazing, if she didn't think about being trapped in some cracked-out Atlantis.

The lights dimmed somewhat. Neva couldn't see around March's body. He was way too tall and broad, and she didn't feel like arguing with him about why he always made her walk behind him. Either he was protecting her, a giant chauvinist, or just oblivious. She decided to give him the benefit of the doubt and picked number three. It also occurred to her that perhaps she'd set herself up for him to automatically shelter her from a frontal assault early in their journey.

March reached back, turning slightly, and grabbed her hand. He bent over so that he could press his lips to the hair covering her ear. He smelled green and crisp as always, and Neva thought about grass snakes and apples. Over his bent back, she could see through the mouth of the corridor into a huge glistening cavern.

"You'll like this," he said in little chuffs of laughter, blowing the stray hairs that had come loose from her knot against her face.

He stood back, his smile wide as the cavern itself, turning his face from glacially beautiful to beatific. She didn't think she could speak without stammering just then, so she kept her mouth shut. March tugged her out of the corridor, down a series out of wide shallow steps of something opalescent and ivory, like mother-of-pearl.

The steps led down to a massive grotto with stalagmites and stalactites of iridescent shell that had grown together, forming round entrances to chambers along the walls. In the center of the cave was a wide pool probably fifty feet across in a wonky shape like an oyster shell. The water wavered and eddied as though fed by running water, but Neva didn't see a waterfall or stream. That didn't mean much, though, because the entire room was a chaos of portals and crevices and different levels of light, all working to confuse the eye. Several people frolicked in the central pool, apparently naked. When Neva tipped her head up to look at the ceiling, she couldn't. The roof just faded into blackness.

"Okay, let go of my hand." March squeezed her hand, and Neva remembered he was holding it. She wiggled her fingers out of his grasp.

He laughed at her, running his abandoned hand through his hair. "I thought you'd like this," he said.

She definitely did. She wanted a bath so badly that there was a good chance that she'd be willing to strip down and just jump in with the others, who were splashing and jumping around like kids at a water park.

A gust of hot, humid air drifted across her face, instantly plastering the hair resting on her cheek to her skin with sweat. "Oh." She turned and looked to her right. The irregular openings into the other chambers stretched away along a curving wall.

"Down there are steaming pools and hot water." She looked back at him. He lifted an eyebrow. "Go on. You'll be fine. No one will bother you."

She was dubious, but not so much that it was going to keep her from what the cavern promised. "It's safe?"

He inclined his head, any trace of amusement gone. "There is no danger here for you. You are one of them. They all recognize that."

"What in the hell are you talking about?" But just like she'd heard the distance chiming when she was still at home, she knew what he meant on an intrinsic level. She'd always belonged to the ocean, never lived more than a mile from either an inlet or the ocean proper her entire life.

He pushed her hair back from her face. "Water calls to water, Neva Jones." March's face fell still and unfathomable, placid like a death mask or a statue. She felt a tremor of awe low in her belly. His hand dropped, and the usual wry twist to his mouth re-emerged, and Neva's stomach flipped over a little at the sex appeal he projected. She thought it had to be intentional, that he had to have seen the effect his expressions and tone of voice had on women for most of his life and cultivated them.

She shot him a glare and turned around, trying to keep her composure. The cavern smelled of salt and that indefinable spa scent that said water. Neva followed the curve of the wall, peeking into the alcoves, the air becoming steadily warmer and more humid. Some of the rooms were tiny and filled wall-to-wall with water, like huge tubs made of shell. Others were so large she couldn't see across them, dark with shifting water reflections on the walls and ceilings. When the air had become so warm she was uncomfortable in her clothes, she began to pass niches colored varying degrees of pink, like the insides of conch shells. She shifted her pack and picked a chamber large enough that three people could easily float around and not bump into one another, with a ceiling tall enough that she could stand up to strip and a ledge large enough to set down her clothes and pack. Tiny steps just large enough for her feet led up into the room and back down into the tub. It was dim inside, dark enough that no one passing by would be able to see her body once she was in the water. The walls were the light pink of a carnation. She toed off her shoes and smiled at the warmth of the shell beneath her feet. The entire room was a superheated steam room and bath, she realized, as it began to lose its definition with the increasing vapor. She dropped her pack, unwound her hair, stuck the scissors in the pack, and stripped off, unselfconscious in the steam.

Once naked, she sat on the lip of the pool and slipped in feet first. The water was soft from mineral salts and smelled like it was the platonic ideal of spa treatments.

Neva laughed to herself with pleasure. Her hair fanned out behind her, and the intense concentration of the salts in the water buoyed her so that she floated effortlessly on the surface. The steam pressed down on her, and her sweat and the steam mingled so that the parts of her body above the waterline were as wet as the parts of her beneath. She breathed deeply, realizing only now that her lungs and mucous membranes had been steadily drying out since she'd left the 98% humidity of Mobile.

Neva floated in the pool and let her mind wander. To relax, she flipped color by color through the rainbow, starting with red, blanking her mind and picturing a series of red objects—a pool ball, a cardinal, her mother's drapes, a Coca-Cola bottle label—until her entire inner eye was filled with the color red. Then she moved on to orange and so on through the color wheel. She'd learned to do this from a self-hypnosis book, but hypnosis had never been her goal. The rainbow visualization was a form of meditation that kept her surface thoughts focused in order to allow her deeper thoughts to shift around and spin up into her conscious mind.

While she pulled up yellow, her subconscious mind took over, threading around the sound of March's laughter, into the shifting trees framing the Ys boulevard that moved in a shifting mass of whispering leaves and choreography like a wave wavering on sand, to Johnson's Beach when she was a kid, to March in the bar in Cardiff with a pint of beer in his hand dressed in regular clothes with his face shuttered and weary.

She drifted off to sleep so gradually she didn't notice the transition. That was always the risk with meditating in the bathtub.

* * *

When she woke she was so disoriented she reached for her alarm clock, struggling up from a deep sleep like breaking free from a riptide. She whipped her hand out for her alarm and smacked only bed. Her eyes were too heavy to open, but she could feel her body cradled in a mattress that was like those ads for memory-foam beds that contoured to your shape. She was sunken down into the mattress—if she had been claustrophobic, she'd be in a panic. The sheets were warm and fluid around her, a luxurious combination of satin and cotton. Her brain came awake before her limbs. She could think well enough to know she was naked and that she wasn't in her own bed. Her mind searched past the Mardi Gras party and remembered the truth of the matter.

Neva forced her eyes open. Above her curved a ceiling in pearly gray and ivory. She pushed herself up on her elbows with great effort, since the bed sank under her with even the slightest pressure. She sat up with her knees almost up to her chest and looked around the room. It was shaped like a huge jellyfish, with a dome ceiling, and a convex floor forming a little knoll. The bed sat at the apex of the hillock and was about the size of two king-size mattresses—and round. The linens were the same color as the walls. March stood silhouetted in an arched doorway clad in nothing but black pants similar to pajamas. He was turned three-quarters away from her talking to an obsequious man who kept sort of curtsying, a very fancy bow, and averted his eyes from March's face. The black of March's pants and hair in contrast to the strange light in the room made his skin appear to glow.

"Hey, get me some coffee," Neva yelled at him. March turned his upper body, and Neva saw the line of his biceps, the sharp line of his collarbone, and his half-lidded smile.

"What do you think I'm doing?" He patted his belly with a couple of loud smacks playfully, and Neva's eyes dropped to his waist, where she could clearly see the sharp delineation of muscle plunging below the black line of his pants.

The servant, or whatever he was, hopped away cringing when March turned his back on him and started across the room toward the bed. Neva let the bed swallow her up a little more, flopping on her back to keep from watching March half-naked, his muscles so defined beneath his skin, shifting and flexing as he moved. His shoulders looked even broader out of his clothes, collarbones standing out sharp. Her mind, however, refused to pay attention to propriety, offering up freeze-frames of his smooth, defined chest and muscled, but not to excess, stomach with that sweep of black hair below his navel. His arms had a starring role in this playback, his biceps cut and twitching as he turned, his wrists thick.

"How did I get here?" She already suspected, but she figured it was best to get those cards right up on the table.

"I carried you. And that was *my* punishment for not mentioning that the waters were soporific." The bed didn't even move as he crawled across it, his voice getting nearer the only warning.

"I'm naked." She wasn't really embarrassed. She was too old for that crap, too immune to that kind of embarrassment after growing up in a family with no real problem busting into the bathroom on a person. She'd lived with two boyfriends and various roommates, and on bad days she wondered if there were even pictures of her naked on the internet.

But it was still weird. She didn't really know him, and he was so young.

"I noticed. You were also slippery from the damned salt. The drugs in the water must work better than I re- member, because I can't believe you didn't wake up when I slipped and yanked your hair." He sighed and his arm flopped across Neva's stomach, with only the sheet be- tween them.

"What are you doing?" Her eyes drifted closed as the smell of the salts in her hair were drowned out by the bright smell of March.

"Snuggling." He yanked his body closer to her, stretch- ing out with his front pressed along her side.

"Hm." Talking suddenly seemed like a struggle. Her eyes dragged closed.

March laughed softly, his fingers brushing hair off her forehead as Neva sank further away from consciousness. "Brown like a crisp fall leaf." He sighed. "Thank you for safeguarding me from Dahut, Neva Jones." His fingers dug into her damp hair, and his leg came up over hers, pressing her even further into the bed.

He began to sing softly, voice clear and strong even in a whisper, like a carillon made of stained glass. His voice chased her down into sleep, and she dreamed of a palace of harps and fluttering drapes sitting on a wide, deep river, of a woman made of flowers with marigold hair and lips of roses.

When Neva woke the second time, it was to the smell of strong coffee and the sound of March's voice. He wasn't speaking English. She had been surprised that everyone seemed to—and had just sort of forgotten how ridiculous this whole adventure had been, with everyone speaking English like a Hollywood movie, or a dream. It was magic, and Neva had no idea how magic worked.

She sat up again and found that the bed was now a more normal firm. Because she assumed March was just sending another servant skittering off on some other errand, she didn't bother to hold the sheet too tightly, and it fell low enough to expose some cleavage. That is, until her sleep-addled brain kicked into gear and she realized that March was fully dressed and addressing another man. He was—oddly—wearing red O.P. boardshorts emblazoned with huge stylized white flowers and a plain red shirt. His shoulder-length black hair was in utter disarray, damp like the others in the city and wildly curling. He sported a deep tan and a black leather wrist cuff.

March had his back to Neva, and the other man watched her tug up the sheet with the sort of mildly stoned, amused expression she associated with surfers.

"Hey, dude, it's all good. Stop harshin' my buzz. Didn't I say it was cool? It's cool. Way cool." His accent was total So-Cal, his voice fractured from salt spray and weed.

March didn't react to his language shift. "Yeah, well, I've heard that shit before, and I know how your moods change like the sand shifting beneath your feet."

"Chill, man, seriously." The man smiled wider, and Neva heard the rush of waves in the distance, heard gulls and smelled the July sun evaporating seawater and concentrating the brine.

March turned his head, and Neva watched his eyes harden.

"If it's cool then lay off." His tone was Neva's third grade teacher's scolding and her mother castigating her in a room full of her peers and red and blue police lights flashing in her rearview. Neva opened her mouth to apologize, even though she knew his ire was directed elsewhere.

The sound of the sea broke off abruptly, and March's face blanked as Neva focused back on him fully.

"Dude, you're so pent up. You need to get laid." The other man laughed and slapped March on the back.

"And you need to spend more time watching over your servants and less huffing nitrous and fucking blonde teenagers." The edge in March's voice was just regular annoyance, nothing paranormal.

"Where are my clothes?" Neva had never wanted to get dressed more in her life. She looked from the new guy's face to March's, and the resemblance was pronounced. March's skin was pale and untanned, but their hair was the same, their eyes different colors but the same shape, their cheekbones and eyebrows almost identical. "Are you two brothers?"

"You know, man, you should stick to stupid betties, because those smart ones will totally jack you up." He laughed again, with a few short wheezes, and March smiled with his half-smile.

"No, we're not." March winked at her. She looked down and next to her were new clothes almost the same as her old ones. Black wide-legged pants and a tunic embroidered at the collar and cuffs and hem. But instead of flowers and vines, stitched in gold, the embroidery was in silver and subtle blues and pinks, forming shells and wavelets. As she watched, the embroidery changed to green leaves and apples.

"I'm Manannan. You can call me Mac." The surfer dude said around a breathless laugh.

March whipped his head around and lifted a finger to point it at him. "Why did you do that?"

Mac shrugged. "I can see where this fucking story's going. Why lie? She'll be mine if you screw this up anyway."

"What do you mean screw this up? It isn't mine to mess up or not!" The heat in March's tone confirmed for

Neva that these two were related somehow. Only family can take you from pleased to pissed in one sentence.

"Whatever, man. Blah blah, yeah, heard it before." Mac swept his eyes over Neva. "She could be it if you don't dick around."

"Can the grand pronouncements. You're on my nerves." March grabbed Mac by the elbow and yanked him behind him towards the archway. "Get dressed," he gritted out at Neva.

Normally, she would have told him to go screw himself for telling her what to do as though he had a right to order her around; as it was, she just flipped him off. He returned the gesture, and Neva almost smiled.

Once March had Mac out of the room, Neva crawled to the edge of the bed, trailing the pile of clothes in her hand, and clutched the sheet around her to look for her knapsack. Oddly, she still felt immaculately clean, without the weird full-body funk that deep, prolonged sleep tended to produce. She found her things and March's piled together next to an alcove in the wall that held a short, stout pot steaming next to a cup as fine as the spine of a sea urchin. Her coffee, obviously, from the smell.

She knelt and rooted around in her pack for a spare pair of underwear. She pulled out a pair of pink boy-legged panties and a lime green bra. Dropping the sheet, she got dressed, wound her hair up, and pulled the scissors out of the pack, sticking them back into the knot.

Pouring herself a cup of coffee, she heard Mac's laughter and the humming burr of March's annoyed voice. She wondered about all of the strange supernatural effects the people here had on her. She wondered if they were fairies, the sort who steal people away and then deposit them back in their old towns a hundred years later without a word. Neva didn't particularly want to go back to Mobile a hundred years in the future, with her family and friends all dead and her house owned by some brassy Yankee family.

"I'm dressed!" She called and sipped her coffee. It was smooth and complex, Jamaican or Kona, which made sense, since both of those places were islands.

March looked murderous, his cheeks magenta and his full mouth pulled into a thin line. The muscle in his jaw ticked. Mac looked pleased with himself, on the verge of laughter. Obviously, Mac was jerking March around.

"Soooooooo, babe, if I asked you for a present, what would you give me?" He pushed his hair back from his face in a motion very similar to March's habit. March glowered at his back with his arms crossed over his chest.

This was obviously more than a hypothetical scenario. Neva glanced from one man to the other. This was a test. One that March was extremely pissed off about. She thought about what sort of answer to give.

She could offer no gift, tell him that he would have to ask formally in order to get one. That was a complex answer, one that assumed a trap. Maybe she was overthinking this.

She could offer the ring she got from King Magog. It was the only thing of real value she had, except maybe the golden scissors.

And when she thought of the scissors, she knew. Her entire quest so far had been for two locks of hair. Obviously hair was some sort of valuable commodity. One she didn't understand, but she had never understood many of the real world economies either. She reached behind her, pulled out the scissors, and untwisted her hair. She pulled it over her shoulder, watching March's arms drop off his chest and his mouth open slightly. Either she was making the worst mistake of her life or doing the exact right thing. Neva clipped a piece of hair about the width of one of her fingers from underneath, where it wouldn't be obvious.

The smile had dropped off of Mac's face while she was absorbed in her task. He stood with his head tilted slightly to the side, watching her steadily. Neva stepped forward and handed him the piece of hair. He hesitated slightly, then reached out and accepted it. Holding the cut end, he stroked his other hand over the six-inch lock of hair before twisting it into a knot to keep the individual hairs together.

March let out a loud sigh. Neva twisted her hair back up, replaced the scissors, and looked at him, hoping for some indication as to whether she'd just doomed him to the inner-most circle of hell or maybe won the lottery.

"I thought you seemed familiar to me, Neva Jones, but I think that was the wrong sort of recognition." Mac's accent still flattened his vowels, but the formality of the language signaled some fundamental shift that set Neva on edge. "For this gift, freely given and unsolicited, I will grant you a boon."

And here Neva sensed a pattern. She smiled.

"Tell me how to free March for good." This seemed like the logical thing to ask. She was on a quest, and apparently this quest had been completed with various levels of competency in the past. Neva figured the best course of action would be to set March free forever. Her granddaddy always said a thing worth doing was worth doing right.

Mac's laughter surprised her. "Neva Jones, that is very simple. Only through true love, freely given, can he be set free. I would think even someone from when and where you hail would know this story." He laughed again, and March sighed again.

"True love?" Neva stared from one of them to the other back and forth. "Y'all aren't serious? That's not something I can just steal or trick someone into giving me." She paused. "Or can I?" She thought about stories where witches kept love in jars. It was possible.

"No, for sure, you totally can't. Sucks, huh?" Mac was back to surfer slang. "Like, listen, when this all tanks? I will hook you up, don't worry."

He winked and made a motion mimicking shooting at her, then walked away, smacking March softly on the face as he went.

"What the hell?" March said nothing in response to her question. *"What the hell, March?"*

"Don't yell at me. What in the hell do you want me to say? That you shouldn't have given your hair? That you're a total fucking idiot!? What? Because right now I'm at a loss over whether to strangle you or go after him and commit a series of crimes against him." He began sounding blasé and worked up to full-tilt screamfest. His face flushed again and he pointed his finger angrily at Neva.

"I don't even know what I did!" She screamed back at him, getting on her tiptoes to keep him from totally menacing her with his height.

"Exactly!" He turned and walked across the room suddenly. "I can't believe you just handed him your hair." His voice came out muffled, his back to her and head ducked down.

She stomped over to him, her bare feet slamming on the cool shell of the floor. Yanking his hand away from his chin, she demanded, "What does it mean? Tell me what I did."

He flipped their hands over so that he was holding hers instead of she holding his. "When you're released from the *geas,* you belong to him now. He can call you to him at will. You gave him an offering, and because you already were under his aegis, that made you his." March's voice bled out strangled, his words tangling up, his statement all hisses and broken off syllables. "I've been avoiding getting wrapped up in the games. Dahut and her Lord have played for far longer than you have any idea of—and you walk right up and ask for a seat at their table! I can't protect you when you act like this."

Neva's whole body chilled, something close to the edge of panic touched her. "How was I supposed to know that?"

"You weren't. The whole Christianity thing is a blessing and a curse, depending on the situation." He sighed, brushing the backs of his fingers against her cheek.

Her brain clicked over and over, not really paying attention to him humming to himself and getting a little too familiar. "What do you mean "Christianity thing"? Who the fuck is Mac?"

"You ask the right questions, just not in the right order." He slid his fingers from her cheek to the back of her neck. His hand could have easily cradled her entire skull.

"That doesn't answer my damned questions, March." The anger was right there, tightening her chest and drying out her mouth.

March blinked at her, pupils dilating as she watched. The blue retreated, leaving black with a narrow rim of color against the white framed by ridiculously long black lashes. "Manannan Mac Lir," March whispered, fingers constricting slightly against her neck.

Neva realized that if her temper hadn't been buzzing and snapping inside her that moment might have been something very different, with March licking his bottom lip and breathing shallowly, such a pretty boy, but Neva's anger was keeping out the fear and the sex, both. She knew that whatever was going on was way more than she'd pegged before they'd arrived in Ys, Lyonesse, wherever they were.

"Should I know who that is?" Neva used their linked hands to push March back slightly, then reached back and removed his hand from her neck. "Hello!" She said as he stood there for a few seconds, apparently stunned with the kind of overwhelming lust Neva understood young men were prey to.

"March!" She barked.

He blinked a couple of times, then ran his hand through his hair, and lifted an eyebrow at her. And that was that, he was back to normal. "Manannan Mac Lir, the God of the Sea, Neva."

"Huh?"

"He has many names, but that is the one he gave you. And I should have known he was up to something." March turned away from her and walked over to the pile where their packs rested. He only picked up his bow and quiver, though.

Neva's mind zoomed around and around, thinking about the stunning resemblance between March and Mac, over her assumptions of their kinship. Her brain sort of short-circuited over whether she should ask the question sitting on the tip of her tongue.

Did she really want to know who March was?

If he was some sort of god he was a pretty lame one,

considering he needed a human woman to come save him. Over and over again. Maybe March was Mac's son? His sort of incompetent, bungling, half-human son? That would explain their dynamic and why March got so angry about Mac inserting himself into Neva's life. Men could get funny about "territory", metaphorically peeing on women to mark them from other men, even if their relationships with the women weren't sexual or romantic.

"If you ask me, I'll tell you." March said from across the room, his head bent down and averted from her. He sounded unsure of himself, insecure, young.

She felt her anger bleed away. "I'm not going to." She had no idea why not other than that he really seemed not to want her to. Whatever reason he had to for that was his business, and Neva didn't feel like raking him over the coals.

He looked up at her, his blank, masking expression on his face.

"How long are we trapped here?" She was hungry.

"Who freaking knows? This place is like the Twilight Zone." He stood up all the way, stretching his arms over his head.

"Oh, that answer's about as reassuring as the fact that you think you need to carry a weapon."

March shrugged. "I never go anywhere without this. You never know when the dolphins are going to riot." He lifted an eyebrow.

"Right. Find me something to eat, mighty hunter." She didn't feel like wearing shoes, and when she looked over at March's feet, she saw he was also barefoot.

March sighed. "All they have to eat here is fish and seaweed. That gets old after a while."

Neva stepped through the archway into the corridor. It was pink and grey and slick to the touch. "You've spent a lot of time here?"

There was a long pause before March answered. Neva could hear his breath and the quiet creak of the leather of his quiver. "Not for a long time." He finally whispered.

"You and Mac fall out?" Neva asked without really thinking.

"No, I've been restrained from acting on my own free will for a long time." Neva realized the wistful tone was probably really sorrow.

"We're going to fix that." She was promising what she might not be able to deliver, but for some reason she couldn't really stop herself.

He laughed in response and touched the back of her neck. All the hair on her body stood on end and her nipples hardened. She crossed her arms over her chest.

Neva wandered the halls of the insane palace/belly of the whale/whatever-that-she-didn't-want-to-know with March at her heels, singing softly to himself.

"Do you know who Jeff Buckley is?" Neva asked him as they stepped into a bustling space as wide as an amphitheater and shaped similarly. He jumped from the top to the bottom of the short set of stairs into the room, and offered her his hand.

She just lifted an eyebrow, and he laughed, dropping his hand. "Sure. I know him."

"Your voice sounds a lot like his." She watched his slowly spreading grin and dimples. "But yours is better."

"Hmmm," he made a mock serious face. "I think you just complimented me."

"I will totally deny it." And why she was flirting with him, she had no idea. She didn't even want to do it. He was just too much, constantly in her space and constantly looking like that and she was only human.

March sang the first few lines of "Everybody Here Wants You." Neva's mouth fell open and went dry. Heat hit her face and endorphins hit her bloodstream so fast she rocked forward, unsteady on her feet.

March caught her arm and leaned against her, lips hovering against her cheek. He sang into her skin, lips slipping and pressing into her face.

Neva held her breath and reached up to touch March's hair. It felt like soapstone and spun dreams under her fingers. His outdoorsy scent sat on her tongue, and she tasted him as he stopped singing and his tongue fluttered out of his mouth to taste where his lips had pressed. She was in a place beyond the shell and the sea that surrounded them, in the two minutes it took March to seduce her she was lost in a way she never would have expected. Cheap trick with the singing, but a woman couldn't really be expected to resist March at all. That was probably the point of him.

He held her on her toes with an arm wrapped around her waist, bending down to open her mouth all the way with his tongue. She twisted up into the kiss, not bothering to be embarrassed at the noise she made when his fingers against the back of her hand flexed and he yanked her into him with too much force.

"No, dude, I really don't think that's cool." Mac's sarcastic, annoyed voice hit her in the spine.

Blinking rapidly, Neva realized that March had leaned away, and her hand fell from his hair. March turned and Neva stepped down onto the floor, watching Mac advance on them with a bottle of Cuervo in his hand, several girls in bikinis trailing in his wake. His voice had broken them apart from across the room, but he had sounded like he was right next to them. Magic. Whatever. Neva's face blushed so hard she thought she probably busted some blood vessels.

Oddly, considering what he'd said, Mac didn't look angry in the least. His eyes blinked heavy, his mouth twisted around into a leering grin. "You always were big with bringing the floorshow, dude." He laughed, and his entourage laughed with him.

Neva couldn't control the annoyed expression she felt slap onto her face.

"Tequila?" Mac lifted the bottle.

"Maybe after I eat." Neva had no idea what the protocol was here about accepting and declining food. She decided to take the giants' manners as the baseline and move on. No way was she going to flat-out refuse anything offered to her, but she also wasn't going to drink tequila on an empty stomach when she'd already almost started making out with March in full view of several hundred people.

"Oysters?" Mac said. He didn't wait for a response. "Oysters it is!" He turned and strode back across the room.

"I do like oysters." Neva shrugged at March.

"Yeah, he knew that." March gritted his teeth. "He knows all about you."

"Is that part of his powers?" Neva didn't know what to do to calm March down. She thought Mac was a total dork, but she didn't think it was the best idea to say that out loud. She slid her hand onto March's back, running her fingers along the edge of his waistband.

He looked down at her with a tiny quirk of a smile, one dimple showing. "You have a serious issue with jealousy, don't you?" she asked. She rolled her eyes and sighed. Boys.

"Yup!" March said, laughing a little, his chipped tooth showing between his pink, pink lips.

"What happened to your tooth, by the way?" She asked, then immediately bit her tongue, realizing that she could have just walked into something bad. Everything here was so fraught with peril.

March just smiled wider, his eyes shifting from bright blue to greenish blue. "Bar fight." He winked.

CHAPTER SEVEN

NEVA AND MARCH were following Mac through the wide, arched cavern when suddenly the cavern transformed into a riotous grotto, like something out of *Girls Gone Wild.* The roof of the cave disappeared—or seemed to—and the sun shone down on a series of swimming pools of various shapes and sizes, each with a swim-up bar and bathing-suit-clad revelers drinking and splashing. Lounge-style lawn chairs sprang up and people fell onto them, instantly reclining and cupping their hands over their eyes to block out the sun.

"What in the frickin' hell?" Neva looked to her left and saw that the ocean almost lapped up into the furthest pool to her left, with just a tiny stretch of white sand between the tiled pool and the saltwater. Overhead, gulls cried and dove. The sky arched overhead. It was cloudless and the watery blue of mid-summer.

"This is new," March observed with a sparkle in his

voice. He looked down at his clothes and they faded, leaving him wearing a pair of black boardshorts with white flowers—a matching set to Mac's—and a black muscle shirt. His quiver and bow were still firmly in place.

"Oh no," Neva moaned, but it was too late. Her clothes also faded, leaving her in a two piece bathing suit consisting of a tank top and boy-legged bottoms in red with hula men emblazoned all over them.

"I guess he has a sense of humor." She looked down at her suit, then up at March. He was smiling, showing all his front teeth, eyes shining, and she felt a little bubble of happiness explode in her chest at the expression on his face.

"So, we're on spring break all of a sudden? Let's roll with that." Neva bumped March with her hip, and he bumped her back. He slid his hand under the knapsack on her back and left it there. She could smell his chlorophyll scent over the seaside smells in the air. It reminded her of home, of long afternoons spent on a beach hemmed in by tall pines and scraggly mesquite.

Mac jumped into a kidney-shaped swimming pool shaded by a series of palm trees along the edge. He managed to keep his bottle of tequila above the water, holding it over his head. Several women jumped in after him, all of them giggling and screaming—except for one, a curvy woman in a pink bikini with bright copper hair. She sat on the edge of the pool with her legs in the water. Mac waded over to her as she produced two shot glasses and a napkin full of limes.

She looked over her shoulder at Neva and March as Mac started doing body-shots off of her thigh. Neva blinked. It was Dahut. The beauty's facial expressions seemed strange, neither amused nor annoyed, just something . . . off.

"What's her deal?" Neva didn't think she had to point out who she meant.

"She's a witch." He said it as though that explained everything.

"Right, and?" Neva shrugged her knapsack off and held it under her arm. March slid his hand up between her shoulder-blades. She turned and walked over to a pool segmented into parts of varying depths, starting off shallowly with long wide steps leading down to about a three-foot bottom. The next segment looked very deep, with more steps transitioning, into it from the shallow part. The third section was of medium depth, and yet another series of stairs led out of the deep part into it. At the end of the medium section a bar was set right into the pool. The multicolored bottles of alcohol rested on a floating bartop, and the bartender was submerged up to his chest, wearing a straw hat and huge sunglasses.

"Is this someplace real?" Neva asked March as she stowed her knapsack under a lounge. She looked up to see March looked down at her, shrugging out of his bow and quiver, smiling wryly. "What?"

"Do you think someone's going to steal that if you don't hide it?" He laughed, depositing his stuff on a chair.

Neva hadn't even realized what she was doing. On principle, she didn't pull her things out from under the chair and put them on the seat. "Habit."

He pulled his shirt over his head, and Neva watched the material peel away from his stomach, then up his chest. She turned away before he got the shirt off of his face, walking over to a series of tables laden with food, similar to the ones in the glass cave they'd been feted in when March and Neva had first arrived. March had been right about the only food available being seafood. Neva, however, had no issue with that.

Trays of raw oysters sat on the octagonal tables that nestled together in varying heights. Open half-shells yawned with pulpy gray flesh, so fresh there was no smell at all. On one of the tables were every condiment known to man. Neva grabbed a small mother-of-pearl dish heaped with horseradish and a shaker of hot sauce and jabbed them both into the ice surrounding the oyster shells. She picked up the enormous tray by the edges and hefted it off the table and carried it over to the chair under which she'd stowed her things. Sitting down, she placed the tray on her lap and dug into the oysters. Applying horseradish and hot sauce to one, she used the fork from the horseradish to pluck the oyster from its shell and pop it into her mouth.

It tasted like the way the ocean smells, with some heat and tang from the condiments. Her eyes fell shut and she chewed with a grin.

"Those used to be the food of last resort for people so poor they couldn't afford to buy fish from fishermen." March sounded disgusted. Neva opened her eyes to see him perched on the lounge opposite her. She doctored up another oyster and ate it with exaggerated pleasure, mocking him.

"I don't know what's grosser, the oysters or the horseradish." His face pulled into a moue of repulsion.

Neva smacked her lips and set about finishing off the dozen or so oysters. March moaned his displeasure and wandered over to the tables to pick at the fish. He picked at a dish of salmon with his fingers, eating a few pink flakes at a time. Licking his fingers, he wagged his head around surveying the rest of the food. Neva could see scallops on their fanning shells, baby squid in a translucent sauce, more oysters, and a white-fleshed fish she thought was probably orange roughy in an egg-based sauce. March polished off the salmon, his clean hand resting on his belly, fingers splayed and beating out some kind of time in no real pattern. He looked at her from under his bangs, smiling slightly around the fingers in his mouth.

"I like freshwater fish," he told her, raising both eyebrows.

"Salmon live in saltwater and fresh." Neva finished her last oyster and set the tray aside, thighs numb from the ice cradling her meal.

"Yes, they do." March snapped his fingers and pointed at her, his grin huge and toothy.

Neva shook her head at him, laughing at his spazziness, and walked over to the pool, stepping on to the steps at the shallow end. The water was only a few degrees cooler than the air, tepid and perfect. She dived under the surface in a breaststroke.

She came up short breaking the surface as an arm wrapped around her waist and yanked her up. "AHHH-HHH!" she shrieked.

March held her against his chest, laughing, tossing his head back and forth, the sunshine picking up the blue in his hair. "You forgot something." He reached into her hair, pulling the scissors out.

"Oh, right. I guess that's why the deer told me to get the gold ones, so they wouldn't rust." She wiggled away from his suddenly slack arms and got out of the pool to tuck the scissors into her bag. March's eyes tracked her movements, and she felt self-conscious. Maybe it was the fact that the bathing suit ended high on her thighs—so high her butt was barely covered in the back—and didn't quite come down to cover her softly rounded belly.

She dove into the deep part of the pool, not reaching anywhere near the bottom on the way down. It was at least twelve feet deep. She propelled off the side of the pool to rocket herself back up to the surface, breaking through and tossing her head back to gasp at the warm, humid air. March sat on the stairs from the shallow end, submerged to his shoulders, raking his hands back and forth slowly in the water.

Neva treaded water, lifting a hand to wipe her hair out of her face.

"The stag told you to pick the golden scissors?" March wore his intense face, and Neva almost sighed. She was sure whatever she'd just said was going to make him revert back into the sarcastic person she'd met by the rocks.

"Yes." She didn't ask why. She really just didn't want to know. His expression hardened further, and Neva opened her mouth to ask him what was wrong against her will when someone hollered "CANNONBALL!" and a huge splash rocked her, sending her under the wake, sucking water into her mouth. She rapidly broke the surface, gasping in air, to see Mac standing in the next part of the pool by the bar. A guy she'd never seen before grinned like a lunatic and swam to the edge to grab a blonde girl by the ankle, toppling her into the water.

Neva figured the party had arrived. From somewhere in the distance, Latin pop music bleated out with a salsa beat. Neva glanced over to March, whose face was blank. She swam over to him and leveraged herself up onto the step above March's, sitting right next to him and leaning back so that she was submerged to the neck, like in a bathtub.

"Are you in a mood now?" She dropped her eyes closed.

"Not in the way you think." March was big on the cryptic comments.

The Spring Break brigade showed up in the shallow end, right on cue, with drinks and lingering touches. Neva accepted her tequila sunrise and watched as two girls in strips of cloth masquerading as bathing suits rubbed at March's chest and arms. She sucked down half the drink in one go.

He turned to her when she let out an annoyed noise. "What?" He raised an eyebrow, pushing the girls away with his forearm. They twittered and swam off.

"They're falling out of their suits." There was no heat in it, more of a dry sarcasm.

March smirked slightly, and looked down at her chest under the water. "So are you."

Neva gazed down and noticed that he was pretty right about that. The top part of the tanktop exposed quite a bit of cleavage at the top, and the sides of her breasts were also probably visible. She rolled her eyes. "That's what happens when a guy picks out your clothes."

"I wish I could laugh at that," March grumped, slurping his drink through a bendy straw.

"Oh, please. Get over yourself." Neva thought March was totally ridiculous with his sudden possessiveness. Such a kid. He might grow out of that, or else get worse with age; she'd seen it go both ways.

"He's a predator." His voice held the edge it had earlier in the caves. Neva watched girls rubbing all over Mac, him laughing with good humor, tossing down shots.

"Yeah, he looks about as dangerous as a frat boy on a bender."

"They're predators, too." March spat at her.

His glass stood empty in his hand when she turned to

him. She curled his hair back behind his ear with one finger and tapped the side of his nose. "You're a saver-type, huh? It's sweet, really. But I've been around a while. I know how to look out for myself."

He snatched her hand up suddenly, mouth quirking. "Do you?" He lunged forward, dragging her with him under the water as she screamed and flailed and lost the grip on her glass. Her eyes popped open in the water to see March grinning right in front of her, tiny bubbles leaking from the corners of his lips, his hair floating around his head like a water-baby. Behind his head kicked a mini-forest of other people's legs treading water.

Neva reached around his shoulders, and his hand moved to rest on her lower back, his smile dimming into something else. She used his confusion to brace her hand on his shoulder, shoving him down with all her weight while kicking her legs hard and propelling herself up. Tossing her head back as she gulped air, she laughed with a sharp, wicked, triumphant spike.

"Totally rad, babe. He wasn't expecting that at all." Mac stood on the edge of the bar section of the pool.

March spluttered to the surface behind Neva. "Hey!" He shouted.

She dragged herself up into the bar area without looking behind her or giving March a chance for revenge. The water came up nearly to her chin when she stood flat-footed. March followed her, mock-scowling when she struggled to run in the water. She gave up on that and swam over to the bar, getting a drink into her hand before March could grab her.

"Look! Drink!" She held it up over her head and slipped the straw into her mouth.

March's upper arms and shoulders were completely above the waterline. He shook his head, sending water flying everywhere, mainly onto Neva's face. "Ah, you A-hole!" She skipped away on her toes, bouncing a little with every step.

"Something strong," March grumbled to the bartender behind her.

The bartender laughed. "She's a cute one, bra." He sounded Hawaiian.

"Hmmmm," March hummed back. Neva wasn't sure how to take that. She got to the edge of the pool and laid her elbows on the rounded lip so that her body bobbed in the water.

March took a sip of his drink and made a startled, comedic face, eyebrows shooting up and nose wrinkling.

"What the hell is this?"

"Banana Fuck-Me Up, bra. Strongest thing I know not straight 151." The bartender took off his hat and trailed it through the water before replacing it on his head. He was blond.

"Girl drink," Neva sing-songed.

March took another sip of his drink, this time without the face. "Girl drink? I think this has kerosene in it." He trudged over to where she floated and mimicked her posture.

"Is it super-sweet and fruity? Then it's a girl drink." Neva kicked her toes out of the water.

"You're drinking something with pineapple juice and a cherry in it." March sounded vaguely wounded.

"Mine's a vacation drink. Different." She punctuated this by noisily slurping her drink.

"Suddenly you're on vacation?" March's laugh warmed Neva's belly.

"Yours can be a vacation drink, too. If you beg." She splashed him with her foot, but had to acknowledge to herself that he was right. She was too at ease here. Why was she trusting any of these people? Why even trust March? She'd never thought of herself as the kind of woman to lose her mind when an attractive man paid attention to her. Was this the effect of the quest itself, the place, the accumulation of magic in her system that she'd wondered over before? Was the magical result that she just accepted what happened easier, stopped questioning the nonsense?

March was quiet for a while as Neva pondered. Eventually, she opened her eyes and tilted her head to look at him. He was backlit by the sun, his expression obscured. He was obviously watching her, though. He looked as thoughtful as she felt.

"You're . . . different." He covered up whatever else he had to say by taking a sip of his drink.

"I feel at home here." And that was the absolute truth, aside from the magical infection issue. The only thing that could make her feel more homey would be a barbeque and some drunken rednecks getting into a fist fight over football or one of their wives. This was a life that she knew intimately, that she associated with most of her good memories. Maybe it wasn't magic so much as the effect of sunshine and alcohol. Hell, it worked for millions of tourists a year, why not her?

"Hmmmm," March replied helpfully. With his odd rivalry with Mac, March was probably not a huge fan of the beach or the beach lifestyle. Which was really too bad, since he was cutting himself out of a world of fun. Neva wondered if he was annoyed at her for being from the coast, if he was pissed that his whole quest had been diverted into some kind of Cancun spring break revel.

Mac started tossing girls into the deep end, one by one, screams and laughter filling the air.

"Fifty bucks says this becomes a topless pool within

ten minutes." Neva rolled her eyes and sucked her drink through her straw. It was strong.

"That's a sucker's bet, baby." He said it BAY-bee, with the emphasis on the first syllable, more of an endearment than sarcasm. Neva cut her eyes to the side of his face. His hair curled against his cheek, tiny drops of water clung to his eyelashes. She balanced on one elbow, the bottom of her glass resting in the water, and reached out to stroke her fingertip over his lashes. His eyes dropped closed. She ran her middle finger over the edge of his eyelid, feeling his eye underneath jittering under the thin skin.

His mouth opened slightly, and before she could react at all, his hand shot up, grabbing her arm. Yanking her hand down, he ran his lips over the veins and tendon in her wrist. The slick slide of his lips on her wet wrist made her lose her balance, and she slipped off the wall, her head ducking under the water. She flailed momentarily, uncomfortable on her back with the surface above her; that felt terror-inducingly wrong. Above the wavering water, Neva could see March staring down at her, his hand still wrapped around her arm. He wasn't smiling. Her world constricted, beating second by second.

March's hand tightened, and he pulled, hard. Neva got her feet under her, and March's other hand came around her waist, pulling her head above the water and feet off the bottom. She kicked her feet back and forth in small eddies, pulling air into her lungs in small gasps.

Bracing herself with a hand on his shoulder, she twisted her arm out of his hand. She made no move to get away from the arm holding her against his body, their breathing synching and the water rocking them closer together. Neva gave up then pretending like she wasn't going to do this. March's face shone bright in the sunshine, freckled with water droplets, his hair black like a curling void against his skin, his eyes almost devoid of irises and half-open, his mouth parted in obvious invitation. His skin slid over muscle under her hand, and March's thigh flexed against hers when she collapsed against him.

"Um . . ." She began. His fingers shoved her tank top up in the back, one finger slipping up her spine. "Yes, but not here." That was about all she could say as her body spun a little out of control, the urge to wrap her leg around his hip and press against him seemed the most logical thing ever in the whole world.

He wasn't listening to her, his mouth dropping to her neck and tongue skipping out to stutter over her skin. His hand on her back pressed up so far it emerged from the top, then slid over to wrap around under her arm, skimming the side of her breast.

And if she were drunker, there was a good chance that she might have blanked out the bacchanal in the pool and let him override her sense of propriety, but instead she shoved at his shoulder and brought her knees up between them. Pressing on his stomach with her knees, she pushed her back against his arm. He tensed his arm, and she realized that if he didn't want to let her go there was little she could do to overwhelm him. His head lifted, and he spun them so that his bulk shielded her from the sight of the others in the pool.

"Okay." His voice fell out of his mouth in shards, his usual timber an octave deeper and the 'kay' not even given full voice, just the hinted tip of it.

He let her go, and Neva's feet dropped to the bottom of the pool. She turned and climbed out of the water by the stairs next to the bar, refusing to look around. Keeping her eyes focused straight ahead, she navigated a path through the labyrinth of deck chairs and tables full of glasses and beer bottles and abandoned plates, around the odd conglomeration of pools, side-stepping running and laughing party-goers. Beyond the palm trees forming the barrier to the pool-zone was a wide stretch of beach. When her foot touched the fine white sand of the beach, March's hand came around hers. She didn't look back.

The beach was deserted and pristine as far as Neva could see. It curved slightly to a point probably half a mile down the shore. To the right, a line of high dunes blocked the view of whatever lay beyond the beach-line. The water rose and fell, teal against the shore, darkening to lapis as the water gained depth, broken up by short stretches of aqua that marked sandbars beneath the surface.

She cut a diagonal line across the beach, putting some distance between Mac's posse and themselves. Neva did her best to focus on the beauty of the water and the beach and not on what she was about to do. When they began to walk slightly downhill, breaking the high tide line, March pressed against her back, his legs tangling with hers and almost tripping her.

He started laughing, the sound as blindingly bright as the sun reflecting off the water. She let her body go slack and his grip loosened, allowing her to break free and run from him, feet digging into the sand, toes throwing it behind her as her feet came back up. Neva ran right into the surf, the sound of the water almost loud enough to obscure March's outraged huffing behind her. She only managed to get calf-deep in the water when March caught her around the waist and lifted her up, her legs kicking, hands gripping his forearms and head beating back against his shoulder.

"No, no, no," Neva laughed so hard she could barely breath, her negation coming out as whispered wheezing.

"Did you think you could escape? Huh? Oh, you are not nearly that fast!" March walked into the waves, his torso shifting against Neva's back, his laughter vibrating through his chest into her spine. He walked them out past the breakers, to a point where the water rocked against his shoulders and Neva knew she wouldn't be able to touch the bottom with her face above the water.

He let her go, and she sank down into water, relaxing, feeling the salt on her skin, familiar and welcome like the smell of her mother's house. Rolling over on her back on the surface, she felt her hair fan out around her head, and used her arms to propel herself so that her toes pressed into March's chest. His half-smile dented the corner of his mouth, forming a dimple on the edge of his lips. She blinked up at him, feeling comfortable and unashamed. His fingers wrapped around her ankle, and she bent her knees as he pulled her foot out of the water, pressing her toes against his mouth. His lips were soft and elastic against the pads of her toes. His tongue zipped out, and Neva sucked in a breath, eyes closing as he licked the water and salt off her big toe. Her eyes opened back wide in shock, and she watched her *Don't Be Koi*-pedicured nail disappear into his mouth. The foot resting against his chest slid off as Neva's entire mind fell out of her head, and her head dipped below the water.

March let her foot drop from his mouth, reaching out to grab her knee. Neva's head crested the inch or so of water it had fallen under as her legs spread about March's waist. He was so wide compared to her that her hips ached at the angle when he pulled her fully against him with a hand under her ass and the other pushing her hair off of her neck and face.

As one of her arms wrapped around his shoulder to rest in the wet curls against the back of neck, she slid the other up the front of his neck to his jaw. She kissed him, pulling his top lip into her mouth and feeling the tip of his tongue against her bottom lip where it moved between his. He tilted his head, and his lip slipped out of her mouth, making room for his tongue to touch the front of her teeth, then slide between them and press onto hers.

Her hand on his neck shot up to grip at his hair, pulling. The riptide caught them slightly. Her feet locked together behind him, and he grabbed her, yanked her hand off of his head and in the same motion shoved her tank top strap off her shoulder. She shrugged out of the other side on her own, the material rolling under her breasts as March wedged a hand between them to press a hand against her chest, moaning into her mouth and pulling back to skate his teeth over her bottom lip.

"We're too deep," she whispered into the shell of his ear, and when he moaned brokenly, shivering, she let out a long breath, purposefully. He shuddered, head lolling back, and wrapped his arm back around her.

He walked them back into shallower water, with his mouth pressed behind her ear, humming. He stopped when the water was a foot or so lower, enough that their height difference didn't prevent Neva from sinking lower, to press against his erection and still not expose her breasts above the water.

She wanted him in an almost mindless way. *Almost.* His bathing suit fastened with Velcro, and she grabbed the front and yanked, March's head falling back and hand tightening painfully on her thigh.

"We can't, you know." She rocked against him. His head snapped back up, and he met her eye. No smile or laughter, just pure want. Neva could almost taste his hormones on the back of her tongue.

"Unlock your feet," he whispered, ducking his face to slip his mouth back and forth on her cheek. She dropped her legs from around him completely, going boneless in the water, and gasped when he spun her around with a hand wrapped around her waist.

The world condensed to the sun drying the salt on her face, March popping the snaps on the front of her suit bottoms, and pressed into her from behind, rocking steadily with a rhythm like the waves around them. His hand slid down her stomach, shoving into her pants, his fingers unerringly slipping to the right spot. His fingers worked in circles as her neck crumpled back against him.

"Oh god." He pulled her hair when that got him even more enthusiasm, his erection sliding against the dent of her spine, his fingers dipping down to slip inside of her before returning to rubbing.

March's face pressed into her neck, and he mumbled unintelligibly. He held her against him with his arm fastened in a vice-like grip around her waist, hurting her, but not enough to make her complain. His face skimming up, lips wetly pressing into her ear.

"Like that?" And his voice did it. Her toes curled and his fingers pressed harder, his hips losing any real rhythm and his arm tightening so that if she wasn't holding her breath he'd have squeezed it out of her.

"Fuck," he moaned, and she scratched at his arm to keep him from cracking her ribs. His teeth raked over the knob of her shoulder, and she pressed her legs together tight, trapping his hand so he couldn't move it.

He relaxed against her, letting his arm drop, and pulling his hand from between her legs. Neva sank down into the water, her feet touching rough, broken shells and slippery sand.

She kicked her feet up and floated on her back, not bothering to straighten her askew bathing suit. Drifting, she closed her eyes, trusting March to make sure the tide didn't pull her out.

"We're both lucky we don't burn in the sun," his voice sounded from directly above her face, and she hmmmmed agreement. A huge hand pressed up against the small of her back—holding her like one does a child first learning to float—and his lips pressed against hers, sideways. She parted her mouth when the point of his tongue touched them. He licked at her bottom lip, then pulled back.

"You're pretty pale," she said finally.

"I don't burn," he reiterated with a laugh lacing the words.

"Because you're a fairy?" She didn't really intend to ask that, but the words just fell out of her mouth. Even with her eyes closed, she could see his smile, in the way his fingers flexed on her back, in the way she could feel his other hand brushing through the ends of her hair.

"You saw the fairies. They bite." His laughter made her stomach flip over. "I suppose I could bite, too, if you wanted."

"Hmmmmmm," she smiled, mimicking the noise he made.

She was a little in love with the sun and the water and March's easy laughter.

CHAPTER EIGHT

THE SAND BENEATH Neva's feet was warm almost to the point of burning as she trudged up the slight incline from the shoreline. They walked back toward the line of palm trees marking the divide between Mac's Cabo-like revel and the tranquility of the empty beach. The shrieking of gulls and the roaring of the tide obscured any noise that March, following behind her, might have been making. She felt strange, dislocated, even more so than when she'd first realized that all of this was real and not some figment of psychosis. Her partying days were long behind her, and she didn't sleep with men she barely knew, no matter how attractive they were.

March's odd combination of aloofness and physicality disturbed her. Neva wasn't the type of girl to see mystery behind a man's silence. Just because a person kept to themselves didn't mean there were hidden depths—just as easily such self-containedness could hide a fondness for Abba or an over-attachment to cars. Added to March's singular lack of sharing was his mysterious connection to Mac and this place. She wondered what she'd gotten herself into *now*. Her mind threw out a freeze-frame of March's curling hair wild around his head, his face cherries-in-the-snow red on white, his sea-blue eyes dilated, one corner of his mouth twisted up into a dimple.

Since March made no move to touch her or speak, she kept her peace and let him be. She was far too old to worry about rejection from a kid who was probably still sowing his oats. She also had too much self-respect to take it personally if he spent a lot of time with women who threw themselves at him at the first opportunity. Why he wouldn't want women to throw themselves at him she wasn't clear on, but she figured it was some odd personality quirk—he liked to work for it, or he thought overly-enthusiastic women were cheap. She didn't want to think about that too much, because she'd rather remember the way his arms felt so solid under her hands or the way his breath tasted in her mouth.

"You hate me now?" March asked from close behind her. Neva jerked, startled. She didn't turn around, though. They were a couple of feet from the tree line, and she wanted to either drink herself to sleep or just pretend like nothing had happened rather than have this conversation.

"No," she answered. Really, what was she supposed to say to that? She felt discombobulated from their rapid intimacy, and the fact that she still had no idea what or who he was. Or if he was dangerous.

"Hmmmmm," March hummed. Which signaled another lack of communicating from him. She felt like they were feeding each other's silence, and she didn't really know how to break that, or how to act.

Neva stepped between two palm trees and onto cement.

Glancing around what should have been the pool area, she sighed. It was completely empty, vacant. No music, no screaming bikini-clad girls, no Mac, no anything but their packs and March's quiver sitting on the ground by Neva's feet. The scene blurred in the middle-distance, the concrete and sky bleeding away into smudges and shifting images.

"Okaaaaaaaaay," Neva bent down to grab her pack, and when she did, she discovered that her clothes were folded neatly beneath it. That was definitely good, because she couldn't really just assume her clothes would be where she left them in a place with no logic she could fathom.

"I'm not going to complain about this turn of events." March swooped over and grabbed his quiver and bow and pack. His clothes were also folded under his things. How his boots had been under the rest of the stuff and could still be standing upright, Neva didn't even attempt to parse. There were serious limits to her knowledge of the laws of physics, she'd learned recently.

March popped the Velcro on his bathing suit and kicked it off with no hesitation, leaning down to pull his pants on. She watched him bend over and step into the legs of the black trousers one foot at a time, the dimples on his back shifting as he moved. He turned to her, as he tied the fly of his pants, shirtless and hair wet against his skin, not smirking or smiling.

"Do you hate me now?" he asked again, and this time she perceived the slightest edge, as though he was trying to keep his voice even, and the effort itself was forcing in strain. His eyes darted around her face, looking for some indication of rejection or ill-ease, she assumed.

March being insecure with himself really seemed like the most ridiculous aspect of a very ridiculous week.

"If I did, would I be ogling you as you got dressed?"

She really didn't know how to deal with March in particular, and with beautiful boys with emotional issues in general, so she did her best to avoid an excruciating conversation about the potentially inappropriate behavior between them.

His smirk let her off the hook for the time being. She turned away from him and hesitated slightly before shrugging and flinging her wet bathing suit off, and rooting around in her knapsack for a new pair of panties and bra. Oddly, the set she'd had on earlier were in there, clean. She pulled those out and pulled them on.

March made a noise behind her. Neva flung her head around, her wet hair flying out and smacking March in the chest.

"Ow!" He rubbed the small, red marks already visible where the ends of her hair had connected with his skin.

"What?" Neva reached for her tunic and pants.

"I've never seen underpants like those." He reached out and ran his finger along the edge of her panties where the material curved with the slope of her behind.

"They're boy-leg." She pulled her tunic over her head. "Comfortable."

Neva was more flustered by the whole underwear thing than the physical stuff between them.

"I meant the colors." March laughed slightly. "But the shape, too. Nice."

Okay, and that was Neva's cue to pull her knapsack on and step into her shoes.

"You've never seen pink underwear? That's just sad, March. You date nuns or old ladies?" She twisted her hair back.

"I don't date."

Neva cut her eyes up to his face, but he was pulling his shirt over his head, so she couldn't gauge if he meant to imply he was the love 'em and leave 'em type or that his lack of social skills impeded him from having a girlfriend. She could go either way on that one.

He strapped his bow onto his back and adjusted his quiver and knapsack while Neva rooted in the pack on her back for her scissors, then tucked them into her hair while watching the gray swirl in the distance.

"What is that? And can I be so bold as to ask you for what we, where I come from, call a direct answer?" Neva lifted her chin at the blurry grayness, even though she didn't think that was necessary. It was best to be specific around here.

"I'm not sure." March sighed. "It could be any of a number of things, but I'm going to go with 'nothing good' as my answer."

"And this is the part where we walk over to it and intrepidly jump in." Neva wasn't asking anymore, she knew that was the only possible scenario, really.

"Normally it would be you, not we, but yeah." Satisfied with the arrangement of his gear, he lifted an eyebrow at her and started walking toward the nothing.

"Don't you know the whole story start to finish? How can you not know what that is? Or what's on the other side of it?" Neva didn't really trust March, not even now—maybe less now that she knew the feel of his muscles shifting under her fingers, the low, growling catch in his voice as he came.

"Look, nothing's gone right since I tagged along with you. This could be a shortcut back into the pattern I know of or it could be a portal to Shangri-la for all I know." His voice rose and fell with annoyance. So things were not changed between them, they both were irritated by each other, and they both lost their tempers. Neva felt more at ease with that.

"Fine." She followed him, walking to his side and then lifting her foot to step right into the future.

A hand clutched her elbow. "What are you doing?" he said, his voice rising to a disbelieving squeak.

She scowled over her shoulder. "Getting on with it."

March's hand slid down her arm to her hand, twisting around to press palm to palm and to wedge his fingers between hers. "We hold hands. So we don't get separated." He raised an eyebrow and scoffed so hard he should have had a thought bubble over his head reading *"MARCH SCOFFS!"*

"Does that really work anywhere but in cartoons?" She was dubious, but he squeezed her hand, and she doubted she could get away from him. She also felt vaguely reassured by him being so insistent on them sticking together.

"What are you talking about? Where did the cartoons come in?" he answered, and she could smell his bright scent over the salt and sea-smell of her own skin.

She took a step forward, tugging him along.

Two more steps and her feet landed on springy grass. She blinked her eyes a few times to clear them of the film that the grayness seemed to have left, and looked around to see that they were in a forest clearing the size of a football field. Pitched all around the glade were multicolored tents fluttering like silk in the breeze. Each tent flew pennants and flags bedecked with symbols that Neva was too far away to make out properly.

A loud wail pierced the stillness of the scene.

"Oh fuck, no." March moaned behind her. He tugged their joined hands to his face, and rubbed the back of Neva's hand on his cheek. She looked up at him questioningly, and he attempted a smirk.

"That bad, huh? Just great," she sighed.

The wail sounded again, and knights in full-on King Arthur's Court regalia swarmed out of the tents running willy-nilly and throwing their hands up in the air like something from a Monty Python sketch. Neva heard the nickering of horses and the blare of a trumpet.

A column of men on horseback charged into the glade from somewhere to the left. The lead man wore light blue shot with gold, his shield resting against his thigh, his reins in his other hand. Behind him three men rode abreast, the middle of whom seemed to be held in his saddle by the two flanking him.

"Just fucking wonderful. First Manannan, now this. My life is complete." He released Neva's hand. His face turned from false humor to hard. His implacable expression that made him appear distant and inapproachable.

"Should I even bother to ask?" She knew it was pointless unless he wanted to tell her what was going on, but her asking him had often yielded results.

March opened his mouth to speak, and out of the underbrush the dog, Cafal, loped, tongue lolling out of his mouth and tail wagging.

"Oh, I suck." Neva said as the dog launched himself at her, licking her face and barking excitedly. "I'm so sorry I forgot you."

Cafal didn't seem to be offended. He bounded around the two of them, wagging his tail so hard he bent in half. March eyed the dog with what Neva pegged as assessment. His look swiveled from the dog to Neva.

"Something strange is happening," he said, voice pitched low and the end trailing off.

Neva's entire body broke out in gooseflesh, the edge of panic making her vision sharper and mind buzz. If March was weirded out, that was a very bad sign.

He pushed his hair away from his face, and held his arm out to Neva, the elbow bent. "Let's boldly face the unknown."

She had no idea what he was talking about, but she slid her hand into the crook of his arm. He pressed his arm down, trapping her hand, and smiled when she pretended to try to jerk it away.

The glade was in complete chaos. Men ran to and fro, yelling and lamenting and ripping their clothes. A clutch of people knelt around a prone figure, all of them with the heads bent, clasping one another on the back and falling against each other's shoulders.

"Someone's badly hurt or dying," Neva whispered to herself.

March rolled his eyes. "You're quick."

More wailing rang across the field. Neva grimaced at the wretchedness of the noise. Cafal bumped into her side, head pressing into her hand. She opened her palm and rested it on the dome of his skull.

March stopped about fifteen feet from the victim and the men kneeling around him. The figure lying on his back was dressed in a red tunic with golden embroidery. The pattern of the embroidery was impossible to make out, due to the fact that the man's insides spilled out of him from a wound cutting from his groin to his sternum.

"Oh, ick," Neva turned her face away, pressing it into March's arm.

The men around the inert man wailed pitifully. Neva could still see the wound in her mind, the grey face of the man drained of blood.

"Are those intestines?" Neva gulped for air, lips moving against the soft fabric of March's sleeve.

"I guess you don't watch *The Operation*." March's light tone and joke jangled, and Neva pulled away from

him to look at his face. There was no smile there, no softness, no softness, no humor. He appeared as hard as his clothes were
dark, beyond her faculties to judge. She felt the strange
awe of him again, like she had in Ys.

One of the men kneeling by the dying figure stood and
crossed the grass to stand before them. He was a sturdy
man, wide and tall, with red-blond hair and a close-
cropped gingery beard. He wore a dark blue tunic with a
dragon stitched on it in white.

"You find us in an inauspicious hour." The man said,
gravel in his voice.

"Isn't that just always the case." March faked an elaborate yawn.

"We hunt Twrch Trwyth," the man continued, looking
up at March with anger plain on his face.

"What else would you be doing?" March spat. Whatever was going on was way beyond Neva. She was annoyed at March for not telling her what to expect.

Two more men broke off from their lamentations and
walk to stand flanking the first one. They were both dark-
haired and wearing green.

"Our king has been grievously injured by the boar."
The man on the left said.

"I'm shocked, really, I am." March pulled Neva's hand
into his and pressed them both against his leg. His bitterness towards these people was not only plain, it was over
the top. Either they were bitter enemies or this was some
choreographed something she couldn't understand.

"You must kill Twrch Trwyth to save our lord." The
man on the right pleaded, his voice raw and cried-out.
Neva looked up at March and felt an adrenaline spike of
fear at the murderous look on March's face.

"I don't have to do anything." The imperiousness in his
tone shocked Neva, but it had another effect on the men in

front of her. The red-head drew his sword and the two flanking him stepped back to give him room to use it.

"You would deny us the life of our king whilst parading your concubine before us?"

Neva blinked. "Concubine?"

"What I do and do not do is of no concern to you. Your king brings his injuries upon himself, as he ever did. How many injuries will he suffer before spurning this pointless quest? A hundred? A thousand? An infinite number?" March released Neva's hand to step towards the drawn sword of the angry knight.

At that point, Neva realized a few things. One, apparently, boars had names, and the one in this story was Twrch Trwyth, which really was a strange name for a pig. Two, March hated either all of these people, or this king person specifically, enough to let him die over it. And three, that she'd walked into another repeating loop of a fairy tale—this one hinging on another quest, saving the king from dying. She had no clue whether this was part of the larger quest for the hair that would release March or another sidetrack that they'd stumbled into. Maybe Mac was watching them from a crystal ball, laughing and drinking tequila.

"You are the only hope to restore our liege's life, and yet you would deny him his this?" The man on the right fell to his knees with his arms up-raised in a theatrical gesture Neva was pretty certain was only going to add fuel to March's anger.

Cafal leaned against Neva's legs, red ears twitching, snout in the air, sniffing, in a protective gesture that Neva recognized from her previous experience with hunting dogs.

March pointed in the direction of the dying man. "Your king forfeited any claim to my aid long ago, Bedwyr. He threw aside the old ways, and for that I will sing at his funeral and have already cursed him heirless."

The two dark-haired men both bowed their heads, ripping at their clothing, but the red-haired man sneered. "You are cursed as our lord is cursed, and that is your punishment for your malfeasance, demon. We will hunt the boar until you are released, and you will heal our king until your hatred is dissipated. Why must you prolong his pain by denying him healing?"

"I revel in his pain, Kei. What he deserves is far worse. A thousand wounds from the tusks of a boar are not enough to assuage my wrath." March stepped forward, and Kei granted no ground.

"What in the hell is going on?" Neva understood the whole curse thing, because, hello, that was the entire reason she was even witnessing this display of penis-size comparison. However, most of the blanks were not filled in, and she was not pleased with the concubine crack earlier.

March turned his head towards her, and when he did, Kei flicked his wrist in a move that Neva read as readying himself to lunge at March. Without really thinking, she pulled the scissors from her hair and whipped them as hard as she could at Kei. They embedded in his shoulder up to the finger loops, and blood immediately began to spread in a livid stain on the blue of his tunic.

Kei grunted slightly, the only indication that he'd been wounded, and pulled the scissors from his shoulder.

"He wasn't going to stab me." March laughed, stepping back towards her and patting her on the back. "HA!" he laughed one massive burst, face lifted up to the sky.

"We should have entreated your lady to hunt the boar for us, Mabon, she is obviously more than your match." Bedwyr inclined his head towards Neva and held his arm out towards her with his palm exposed.

"This is not her quest," Kei wiped his blood off of Neva's scissors, leaving two smears across the body of the white dragon on his tunic. "But I would offer her a place in our party." He turned the blades of the scissors towards himself, sheathed his sword, and offered the finger loops to Neva. She accepted them and tucked them back into her hair.

March watched her steadily, eyes unblinking, "Well? Do you want to go hunting, concubine?" He lifted an eyebrow, small smirk on the corner of his mouth.

"I thought you didn't want to help them." Now she was really confused. March was far too mercurial.

"I don't, but I do want to see if you can really ride a horse." His smile bloomed fully, exposing teeth and dimples. "I didn't believe it when you told me you could."

He was teasing her, and she wondered what it meant that he would help his enemies in order to play a joke on her. From the corner of her eyes, she saw Kei looking between the two of them.

"I've never even seen a boar before." Neva wasn't sure what she found more disturbing, the fact that March was actually something of a hard-ass bastard or that she was extremely attracted to that.

Neva stood next to the huge red horse, looking it up and down. The horse eyed her in turn, its brown eye blinking and looking away as he shook his head and whinnied.

"Where's the stirrup?" She had the feeling she'd yet again agreed to something that was far more complicated than she'd realized at the time of agreement.

"Introduced later." March ran his hand over the blanket sticking out from under the saddle on the horse's back.

Introduced later was an interesting phrase. It implied

many things, one of which was that somehow they were sometime before stirrups had been invented; on the heels that idea was the one where they were in the past, and following swiftly upon that was the concept that they were somewhere real at all.

March's eyes settled on hers, and she knew that if she asked he wouldn't lie. How she knew that was up for debate, but it was probably magic, just like everything else in the last few days. Or it could be that there was something real between them, some kind of fundamental understanding.

"We're somewhere real?" So many things were wrong with that. The first was that she could speak to the Bedwyr, Kei, and that other guy and if they lived before the introduction of the stirrup in the British Isles, that was impossible because they wouldn't be speaking English. However, the word impossible had sort of lost its blush.

March shrugged and rolled his eyes. "What does *real* mean?"

Neva rolled her eyes back. "Real means on planet Earth and really happening, not a dream or in some alternate reality."

March's mouth twisted into his half smile. "That isn't at all what 'real' means. Real means that a person can accept something as happening at all, that their mind doesn't reject it or ignore it."

"Are we going to believe Tinkerbell back to life now?" She knew that she had no point to argue from, considering everything else, but sometimes March just made the stupidest comments, and she suspected they were intended to goad her into annoyance. He was a shit disturber.

"Dreams aren't real? How do you know that's true? Haven't people speculated since the dawn of time that dream-life is realer than waking life?" His smile grew, and she knew he was teasing her, but not exactly how. He was pleased with himself, and she still had no answers.

"So this isn't the true story that King Arthur or the Fisher King sprang from, like, historically real?" That thought had been tickling at the back of her mind like a half-remembered name ever since they'd seen the wounded king.

March's smile turned sharp on the edges, and his eyes dilated slightly. "I didn't say that."

The black against white against black of his tunic and hair framing his face made his lips and the spots of color on his cheeks bright red, like blood on snow. His lips parted, the bottom one gravid with blood, the top bowing up in invitation. Neva's pulse beat against her wrists and neck so hard she expected to look down and see spots of blood smudged on her skin. March's eyelashes fluttered against his cheek as he stepped forward, hand up-raised, and hummed in the back of his throat.

Neva thought of a pristine pine forest at night, the crisp air of midwinter mixed with pine sap and wonder, of the endless hope of youth buoyed by unrealized innocence—she knew it was all March, the smell of him and the way his nearness seemed to ring something ineffable in her. She felt like she was seeing a new color for the first time and realized that maybe that was the feel of magic on her, that what made March irresistible was the fact he *was* irresistible.

He leaned down, his thumb brushing her cheek and his own cheek rubbing against the other side of her face. "You are hazelnuts and oak leaves underfoot." His murmured words bled through her skin, burning and intoxicating like whisky after a long thirst.

She ran her fingertips over his eyelids, down his nose,

and onto his lips where she slipped them back and forth until his tongue darted out, soft and warm. March stood back, his hand still on her face, no smile evident.

"This is the story that others came from." He looked upwards, and Neva had a hard time remembering why he was bothering to talk, where they were, and why they had their clothes on. "It's really complicated in that way where things are when they're unexplainable, because half of the explanation needs five other things explained first. This is the story that spawned all the other stories like it, all the tragic stories of the dying king, of the star-crossed lovers who loved truly and brutally and were sundered, of the great betrayal of someone of true purpose and heart by someone he loved."

"Um, yeah, don't go into teaching." Neva reached up and rested her hand over his, pressing his fingers more firmly into her face.

He raised an eyebrow and grinned. "Your language leaves a lot to be desired. There are words you don't have in English, all right?"

March was suddenly dropping information like water through his fingers, telling her things she never would have thought to ask, and her stomach flipped over at the implications to that. Would he have to dispose of her somehow now? Keep her trapped forever? Would she care if she did have to stay?

"Whatever, English has the largest vocabulary of any language ever."

His hand slid down her neck to her collarbone.

"Having more words doesn't mean having the right words, okay?" His smile broke through his serious mood. Without warning, he dropped to one knee, laced his fingers together, and looked up at her. "Hop on board."

"You could probably just pick me up and put me up

there." She lifted both eyebrows and planted her hands on her hips.

"Oh, so now you're Miss 'Just Do It For Me'? I thought you had principles and all that crap," he lifted his hands toward her, mock scowling.

"When did I say that? I think you assumed that because I'm not completely incompetent and I don't expect you to save me from breaking my nails and getting dirty." She stepped into his hands with her left foot and planted her hands on his shoulders, and almost screamed when he dropped her foot and stood in one fluid movement, grabbing her in a fireman's lift and swinging her around to plant her on the back of the horse.

The horse stood placidly, munching grass as Neva emitted a high-pitched whine and March laughed loudly enough to pierce eardrums.

"Hey!" Neva slumped forward, almost laying down over the horse's neck.

March's joy spread through her, though, the sight of his hair flying around his face and his eyes wide-open commanded her mouth to soften and turn up.

"So you know how to use the reins? Because I can ride behind you . . ." March started, but broke off when Neva kicked out at his head. He caught her foot and shook it back and forth.

A throat cleared behind Neva, and she circled her mount around the see what was happening. She had to clutch tighter than she was used to with her knees, and knew her thighs were going to be killing her in short order. Bedwyr stood holding the reins of a black horse with a white crest on its forehead, looking scandalized.

"When my lord and my lady are prepared to travel . . ." March cut in. "Save it, we're ready."

His tone when he spoke to the knights was one she

couldn't really pin down. It was neither anger or agitation, really. Maybe it came closest to a weary parent castigating a disappointing child. March led over a dappled grey horse, and looked up at Neva with his blank expression as he passed her. She followed behind him, watching him mount his horse with the sort of inexplicable agility she should have been unsurprised at by this time but was still stunned by. Looking back over his shoulder at her, he smirked. She rolled her eyes.

The woods around them chimed and bustled with wind, the calls of unfamiliar birds, and the chittering of wild creatures. Neva breathed in the unpolluted air, the taste in her nose and mouth the way water in a clear spring looks—reflecting everything and nothing, fluid and the same yet always changing—and she listened to the knights discuss crop yields and the pedigrees of cattle.

"They don't seem too worried." March's face was averted three-quarters when Neva spoke. He held his reins loosely in his left hand, pressed against his thigh, in a very comfortable and familiar way. When she fell silent again, he tilted his chin down and swiveled his head so he could look back at her, where she rode behind him. The woods were full of paths wide enough to ride two abreast, clean of leafy detritus. Neva had decided not to bother wondering about that, all other things considered. Naturally in the Original Fairy Tale the paths were clear and wide enough for people to ride abreast.

March's face, framed by the softly whispering foliage and his winged curls, looked as close to the definition of haughty as she'd ever seen outside of one of her mother's society functions. His slightly up-turned eyes fell half closed in indolent boredom, and his sybaritic mouth dimpled at one corner above his lifted chin. He cocked an eyebrow, and the look was complete—the too-beautiful villain in a swashbuckling Errol Flynn movie, or the overblown drawing of a pagan idol on a tarot card.

"They trust me." His voice carried nothing, emotion or even a hint of an accent. Neva wasn't sure he was even speaking English. Her skin froze, then burned in a sudden bout of panic.

"They trust you to what?" Her mount came fully even with his, and he lifted his hand to tuck her hair behind her ear, leaning over steadily in his saddle, face remaining static, immobile. Her fear did not abate with his familiar behavior, his familiar, almost possessive behavior, as the backs of his finger ran down her cheek.

"To save their king." The words dropped from his mouth like wrongly struck notes, discordant and flat.

"What's going on?" She was swallowing her heartbeat and watching her ability to read March fade subtly, like increasing blindness at dusk.

"What question are you asking?" Blinking slowly, March tilted his head to the side, watching her.

Neva really didn't know the answer to that. Was she asking him about the newest prong of their quest, or why he was acting like a freak? Was she asking him some larger question about life? Somehow she knew that March probably held many of the answers to imponderable questions that people had struggled with since humans stood upright and waded through the tall, sweet grass of the savannah.

"Have you done this before?" Neva had no idea why that was the question that threaded its way out of her mouth.

His eyebrow lifted again, and the corner of his mouth followed, twisting up in a smirk that felt like the end of a bitter winter, like something that Neva had been waiting for her entire life but never knew it. It was the magic again, maybe, or something she didn't want to think about, something emotional.

"This is one of my first stories." His smirk lit up, his face bright and red-cheeked, his eyes peeping bright, and his mouth opening to show his chipped tooth. "Do you like pork chops? Because I *love* them!" He threw his head back, exposing his white neck in a long, vulnerable line, and laughed, shocking birds from the trees.

"I see the oblique thing is just to amuse yourself." Neva rolled her eyes, but felt the laughter straining in her throat.

His chaotic laugher subsided into chuckles. "Not really. Sometimes that's accidental. Or brought on by anger." The second part was pitched lower, meant just for her.

Neva watched the backs of the knights ahead of her. They chatted and joked, seeming at ease in their saddles and with March and her at their backs. Their camaraderie appeared deep and substantial, based on things Neva knew nothing about.

"They aren't romantic hero-figures." March's voice gritted around the sibilants just as the path they were following opened out into a wide glade where tents already stood erected.

"I wasn't thinking that," Neva shot back at March. His blank face told her he was hiding something.

"Maybe you weren't now, but maybe you just haven't yet." March swung down out of his saddle and covered her hands with his. When Neva moved to run her thumb over his palm, he extracted her reins from her hands and looped them over her horse's head, leading her mount—and her—into the glade. "Every woman's read a romance about a knight."

"I haven't," said Neva, even though she *had*. "Why are you being so insufferable?" She wasn't really annoyed, just tired of him changing mood second to second so that she could never relax. He kept her constantly on edge, waiting for the next shift, the next game or trick.

"This is a story I've lived more than once, this is *the* story that began this all, but the last time the one wounded by the boar was me, Neva, and the one who caused that is now lying broken on the grass, and I have the feeling that that's important."

CHAPTER NINE

NEVA FOLLOWED MARCH into the clearing, wondering what it meant that she believed without reservation that he'd lived these events before. It certainly explained his attitude toward the knights and his general haughty demeanor. She watched him ride a little away from her. Her mind jumped from question to question. Had March been their king? Had he been the star-crossed lover or the betrayer?

In the field, tents clustered and sprawled in a way that jived with her childhood imaginings of Camelot. A rainbow of brightly-colored silk fluttered in the wind, pennants and the tents themselves trembled in breezes that Neva didn't feel. Horses were corralled in a series of paddocks near the right-hand side tree-line. Knights and women in dresses and in loose trousers and tunics like Neva's clustered around fires or the mouths of tents, drinking and eating and generally not at all acting as though anything dire had transpired. The whole atmosphere reminded Neva of the pictures of people during the Civil War at Bull Run picnicking and frolicking while canons popped off in the distance.

"This is weird." Neva relaxed her thighs and wiggled around in her saddle. A man strode over to Kei, who was ahead of them near the closest paddock, and he wagged his head when Kei made various gestures towards Neva and March. The guy started toward them. Neva thought about getting down from the horse's back and tried to gauge how she was going to accomplish that without a saddle horn to grip or a stirrup to balance on.

"Help down?" March blinked at her slowly and smiled slightly.

"Maybe," she said, sniffing in feigned snobbishness. "If I allow you to help me." She was at a loss as to what to ask him, how to ask him important questions that he would answer directly and not in the oblique way he had learned to fend her off.

March laughed, swinging down from his saddle with the same economy of motion he'd used to get into it. He dropped his reins, and his horse wandered in the direction of the paddocks, in no apparent hurry. A stablehand grabbed the reins of March's horse as March reached up to wrap his hands around Neva's waist, tugging her toward him and then onto him. She just collapsed and let him pull and clutch her before setting her down on her feet.

"That was weird. I'm not used to being manhandled like a little kid." Neva adjusted her hair, bumping into March's chest. He made no move to step away from her. His shadow engulfed her, and his woodsy smell sank into her. She stepped back from him, but before she could complete the move, his hand wrapped around her elbow to hold her still.

Behind her, she could hear her horse being collected by

the stablehand in a tinkling of reins and whinnying. March looked over her head, his face burning red high on his cheeks.

"Something's wrong here." He whispered so low that Neva almost asked him to repeat it, her brain taking a second to register the words. Neva watched his eyes track over the campground pausing to catalog features she couldn't even speculate on.

She definitely agreed that something was wrong here. Not the same something, though, she was sure. Neva was out of her element in this world.

"Why did Bedwyr call you Mabon?" Neva thought then was as good a time to ask possibly difficult questions as any. The stabler had wandered away with their horses. No one else was around, and who knew how long that was going to last.

March kept scrutinizing the scene behind her, and she kept watching him.

"That's what they call me." He paused, mouth turning up slightly. "Obviously."

"Uh huh. Is it your real name?" Fairytale princes usually had a secret name. Neva wasn't an expert, but she'd seen a Disney movie or two.

"It's an old one." His eyes dropped suddenly to her face, and the odd dissociation fell over her again. She felt the edge of euphoria and the hum of lack of oxygen and something with no name at all. His eyes darkened, and he seemed to loom even taller, impossibly huge, filling the whole of the sky.

"Is this magic?" The words came with difficulty, falling back into her mouth when she tried to speak them.

March sighed, and Neva breathed it in. March's breath in her lungs became her whole world, collapsing all thought and self into a wide-open *beyond*.

"I have waited a long, long time for you, Neva." She tasted the words, felt them embed in her skin, smelled pine sap and thin air in them, saw them in the aquamarine infinity of March's eyes.

Love was a word for fourteen-year-olds and for her mother. What Neva felt for March had no name. It was her first realization of the existence of the impossible, the ever-vanishing ground in an infinite fall, the incomprehensible.

A commotion began behind her, and whatever freakishness had just happened snapped with a tangible crack. March's grip on her arm tightened painfully and he pushed her behind him so hard she stumbled and almost fell.

"What the hell?" she shouted at him as he began trotting toward a riot about a hundred yards from them near one of the tents. The light blue silk of one of the men's tunics was stained in a large splatter pattern that Neva could see even from where she was glaring towards March's back.

She started after him just as he turned and shouted towards her. "Stay there!" He gestured emphatically. That sealed it—Neva sped up, fuming and ready to hit March in the head with whatever was handy when she caught up to him.

What an idiot he was, really. A very strange and probably dangerous idiot, but she didn't really care if he had some kind of voodoo, he wasn't going to tell her what to do or toss her around like some kind of doll. She was sure that he needed *her* to escape from this lunatic asylum. She stomped after him, getting caught up in the hysterical crowd and losing him in the throng. Knights and women jostled Neva and paused to stare at her when they caught sight of her. She ignored them and shoved through the bodies, intent on finding March and hollering something really incendiary and scathing.

She worked her way through the people until a ring of men standing shoulder to shoulder prevented further progress.

"Hey!" She tugged on the tunic of the man standing in front of her. He turned his head and glanced at her over his shoulder with a raised eyebrow. "I'm with . . . Mabon." She thrust her chin forward and made her face as hard as she could manage.

The man blinked dark eyes behind black lashes. He twisted his body slightly, making a gap for her to shimmy through, indicating with his hand that she had his permission. His silence was unnerving in the tumult of a shouting crowd. Neva wiggled through the gap he created.

When she emerged from the press of the crowd, she was standing on the edge of a ring of men. Inside the circle stood March with his bow in his hand facing a large hairy pig with tusks.

"It has been many seasons, Bright One," the boar said.

Neva's mouth fell open, but only for a second. She realized that it was only logical, according to this place, for the pig to talk. He had a name after all, Twrch Trwyth.

"Destiny is such because it's inescapable," March's voice carried, even though he was obviously pitching it just for the animal.

The boar wasn't dark brown or reddish as she would have expected. His bristles and hair were a pale color, close to towhead blond, maybe white, and his skin was pinkish. He was massive, probably over five feet long, and stood as high as March's waist. A press against her leg told Neva that Cafal had found her. She dropped her hand onto his head and touched the thin skin of his red ears, and he pressed harder into her side, leaning all his weight on her.

"One must die so another may live, as a snake eating its tail," the boar responded after a lengthy pause. Snakes again. "I will die as you betray me for those unworthy, those who breath oaths. This is our tragedy, beloved boy."

Neva took a step forward as the men in the circle began grumbling and shifting. March threw his head back, mouth open in what could have been a silent scream, face twisted into grief and anger so horrible that Neva picked up her pace and jogged towards him with Cafal at her heels nipping at her clothes in warning. March reached behind him and pulled an arrow out of his quiver and strung it in his bow, lifting and aiming in a fluid, natural motion. The boar lifted his tusks and turned and ambled away slightly, positioning himself so that his left side was to March.

Breaking in a dead run, Neva shouted "No!" alarmed in a way that made no sense, but killing a sentient animal seemed wrong to her in a fundamental way, and March was so upset. The boar, when he lifted his head to meet her eyes, was intelligent and aware. Cafal lunged into the backs of March's knees as Neva hit March in the back, intending to knock his bow aside.

March rolled to the ground, his bow flying off somewhere. The boar galloped off, running right past Neva and ducking his head at her. She stretched her hand out, bringing away several, long white hairs. Men flooded in around them, screaming and running and waving weapons. Cafal snapped at anyone who came near Neva. She rolled over and scooted on her hands and knees towards March who was flat on his front on the ground. The arrows in his quiver lay flung on the grass next to him, and his head was turned away from her.

"March." She grabbed his shoulder and tried to roll him over. When that didn't work, Neva climbed over him and leaned down to see his face. His eyes were open and his cheek was pebbled with flecks of dirt.

"Are you okay?" She tried to push him over by his

shoulder. He blinked at her. When the corner of his mouth cracked open around a broken grin, blood showed in the gap. Her heart stopped beating entirely for several seconds, her breath stilling in her lungs and her pulse one long painful throb when she finally felt it against her temple and wrists.

People streamed around them, and several chorused *Mabon*. The rest of their words failed to register. March's fingers flexed slightly in the grass. Neva reached down and grabbed his hand.

"Roll me over." March coughed and wheezed out the words, and Neva felt panic stealing her higher brain functions. She was suddenly looking at the world from far, far away. The hands that grasped March's bicep, that wedged under his ribs and hefted, couldn't have been hers. A dog's tail kept wapping the side of a face that certainly didn't seem to be hers.

Protruding from March's chest, when he settled onto his back, was the broken shaft of an arrow. He leaned up and looked at it, smile widening before he began a rattling cough.

Neva reached down to grab the arrow. March's hand settled around hers. "No." When he coughed again, blood hit Neva's cheek. She didn't bother to wipe it off.

His hand turned hers over, and she saw that in the middle of her palm was a tiny golden key. March's head dropped back on the grass with a whoosh.

"I'm *dying*," March said through a blood-stained laugh. "I'm dying." His eyes met Neva's and her panic turned to terror. She blinked and felt the burning rush of tears threatening.

"But you can't die, can you?" She didn't know why she thought that, but it seemed right and reasonable in a way that it couldn't have been for anyone else.

Blood made the front of March's tunic slick and a different black from the dry fabric, shiny. When he grabbed her other hand, the one without the key, he smeared red fingerprints all over her skin, sticky; the smell hit her—copper and salt—and she could *taste* it against the back of her throat.

"Beautiful irony," March gasped. "My life for Twrch Trwyth after taking his . . ." He tried to roll on his side, but didn't quite make it. ". . . so many times." He let out a low moan that set Cafal off whining.

Neva's brain tried to kick back into gear. "You killed him more than once?" She paused as March nodded slightly. When she closed her hand around the key in her palm, she felt the edges bite into her skin. "And he came back to life?"

"Come here." March gestured to her with a curl of his fingers. He lay crumpled up on his shoulder, curled in on himself and struggling to breathe. Neva dropped down onto her side, with Cafal immediately pressing into her back and resting his head on her shoulder to stare down at March, and March resting his forehead against hers.

"I'm sorry," he sighed, starting off on a coughing fit. She thought he probably had a collapsed lung from the rasp and gasp of his breathing. She was about to ask him why he was sorry when he pressed his bloody thumb into her mouth.

She tasted salt and copper and felt a brutal dislocation, like walking through a waterfall. She was no longer on the ground with March bleeding to death next to her, with aimless men milling around and shouting ineffectually. She was zipping through the air, as if in a dream.

Neva hadn't ever had dreams about flying like so many people she knew. She had had dreams about being on television shows and eating food she didn't like. Sometimes she dreamed about falling. But what she experienced now was better than a dream. It felt real, like a cramp in her leg or the taste of watermelon-flavored candy or the sound of a gunshot in the distance. Her body zipped through the air, her face stinging from the wind slapping her and clothes fluttering around her. Because it felt like the thing to do, she shot her arms out in front of her like Superman, and that kept the wind from hurting her face, and WOW. She had nó idea what was happening, but it was better than . . . when she remembered March laying on the ground, with blood pooling next to him on the grass and the natural paleness of his skin bleaching to ashen pallor, she dropped her arms and fell in a series of somersaults toward the ground. Or toward what she assumed was the ground, because she was spinning too fast to see.

A hand shot out and arrested her mid-spin, and gravity and centripetal force rocked her bones in their joints. Her feet hit the ground, and she blinked up into March's smiling face. His smile was so huge that it looked like it hurt.

"Um." She had no idea why she was shocked, because, really, this was just par for the course. He wasn't bleeding or hurt or anything that meant death. He stood right there in front of her with his eyebrow cocked and hair flying around his face, huge grin collapsing down into a smirk. "What the fuck's going on?"

"You're filthy." He licked his thumb and rubbed at her chin. Behind him was a stretch of forest that looked neither sinister nor remarkable in any way. He leaned down, thumb flowing down her chin and against her throat, and brushed his mouth back and forth over hers until she flicked her tongue out to touch his bottom lip. He was trying to kiss the questions out of her, and he wasn't even subtle about it. Tilting his head to the side, he slid his tongue into her mouth, making a, low humming sound and then turned frantic—fingertips hard and insistent, arm coming around to lift her up against him, mouth devouring and wide.

She felt the disconcerting awe creeping over her, feeling wonder and ecstatic fervor just to be near March. He moaned loudly and broke the kiss to press his face into the juncture of her neck and shoulder. "Oh, please," his voice fell through her skin, begging and ripped up. He let her slide back fully to her feet and sank to his knees with his face pressed into her stomach, arms wrapped around her too tight and bruising her slightly. She let go and let the bliss and insanity rush in, falling into his adoration and not caring anymore that it probably meant he was manipulating her somehow.

A series of images skittered through her mind, starting with bright yellow light so intense it should have burned out her eyes—instead the light felt comforting, comfortable. The light faded and a great hall of shining marble with floor to ceiling windows appeared in the vision. Faces appeared, men with raven-wings for eyebrows and women with wisdom in their eyes.

Neva *became* March. She didn't know how, but without hesitation she knew her thoughts were now his. The feel of grass under her bare feet and the laughter of the birds overhead filled her mind, big and profound and perfect, perfect. The pleasure and completeness was endless. Her smile fit on her face the way the sun fit the sky.

"We love you, Lord, we love you and do all in your name, we worship you with our hearts open and expect nothing but your love in return," several voices twined together, one word spoken by one then the next another, the warp and weft of many hearts joined in one acclamation.

The sun felt heavy and liquid on her skin, pressing her

and holding her. Sunshine and love and the shiver of the woods after an easy rain. The sun dimmed slightly as a figure stepped into her line of sight, wooden sticks in a cross slapping against his chest as he moved.

Betrayal so deep her bones felt like cracking obliterated all ability to think. There was nothing but pain and the deep sadness of someone who has had love and felt it ripped away, all the memories replaced with lies. The endless summer wiped away in one cataclysmic autumnal moment.

Several men in leather armor looked at her with hard faces. "You're a devil," they chorused. Her heart blinked out.

The slick warmth of March's hair under her hand was the first real feeling of her own she had when the images stopped. When she sucked in a breath to speak, he yanked her down by her hips, and she willingly fell into his lap.

They turned their backs on me, tried to hand me over to their new priests. But they were fools and idiots, because no man has the power to bind me. His words dropped right into her head, like her own thoughts, but in his voice.

"You're a god?" She was starting to lean back to toward the "being insane" theory that had gotten her into all of this in the beginning.

Some would say. Some would say demon or angel or some other name that has no meaning to you. Even in her mind, he sounded amused. His mouth turned up, as his hand slid from her hip to her waist.

"Where are we?" He was suffocating her with his expectations, and she wanted to let him, to give him whatever it was he wanted, because no matter what he said he was, she had seen him bleeding to death on the ground, his own arrow in his chest.

In a place that isn't. In my mind, if you want to think of it that way.

"You're dying." His smile deepened when she said that. "How can you die if you're something bigger than human?" Because that just didn't make any sort of sense that her brain was willing to accept.

I have seen others like myself pass beyond our world or yours. What happens to them is as opaque to me as your own death is to you. I do not like what my existence has been these mean seasons, but I do not want to pass beyond what I've always known. His smile dropped from his mouth, and his hand clutched at her. She scooted closer to him and wrapped her arm around his shoulders, pulling him against her.

"What can I do?" She pressed her lips to his ear and wondered which was crazier, that she was pretty much sure she was completely in love with him, or that she didn't even care if it was all real or not.

Find Twrch Trwyth and ask him for counsel, because this is not my story. Ever before, since the day when the man I trusted the most, loved with all my heart and gave immortality to, out of a desire never to be without him, betrayed me and set this series of curses into motion, I have killed Twrch Trwyth to save my oath-breaking friend. As he spoke in her mind, Neva saw the bright smile of March's companion, the original king who became Arthur and the Fisher King and so many others in the myths of mankind.

"I won't let you die." They both knew she was lying, overextending herself, but that made his kiss all the sweeter, the taste of March's tongue against hers something close to forgiveness in advance of failing.

She shoved him back and he lay down, pulling her down on top of him, sliding his hand down the back of her pants. Her legs fell open, straddling his belly, and it was awkward because of how tall he was. Awkward but vital with the possibility of *never again* pressing them into each other and the ground.

March rolled them onto their sides, and as they rolled, Neva gripped the waistband of his pants and tugged, pulling them down one hip. One of March's hands kept her face off the ground, cradling her cheek as he kissed her, and the other yanked at her pants in an echo of her own actions. Blink, Neva bit March's lip, blink, his teeth raked over her chin, blink, his hand was against her, rubbing, and her pants were gone. She fell back, pulling him by his arm and his hair, her knee slipping against his hip, her foot pressing on the back of his thigh.

There was no hesitation, nothing but the absolute certainty that the world would cease to exist if March's weight didn't break her a little, if his hips didn't force her own so wide that they ached slightly, if he wasn't frenzied and not as dexterous as someone who had lived so long and looked like him should be. The shocks of pain and the stuttering of his rhythm inside her made it more *real*, more just March, who wasn't perfect, just maybe as close as it was possible to get.

She tugged at his tunic, and he leaned back to let her yank it over his head, hair even wilder when his face fell back to hers, lips skittering across her cheek and pressing into her hair, against her ear. The ability to think left her when he shifted his weight back and thrust his hips so that he hit everything possible to liquefy her mind. Her fingers pushed and pulled and grabbed, and when he groaned around a smile, she whited out, closed eyelids reflecting his half-lidded wicked face.

Neva blinked her eyes open, the lids beating back and forth, refusing to work correctly. The metallic tang of blood made her tongue feel thick in her mouth. A wet cough made her snap her eyes open fully. March's dilated pupils and ragged smile, exposing his chipped tooth, made her squeeze her legs together. The blood seeping through his fingers where they squeezed around the arrow shaft in his chest made her stomach flip over.

"Kiss me," he mouthed, not enough breath behind the words to be even a whisper. She felt the plump resilience of his mouth against hers, and his tongue brushed hers open even as he lay within death's shadow, bleeding over both of them. He choked on a cough, and she pulled back, wiping the blood from his face with her sleeve. His eyelashes curled against the slope of his cheek, his red lips all the redder with his face so pale—he was still so beautiful even now.

"I'm going to frickin' save your ass." Neva brushed his cheek with a finger and stood up, Cafal leaping in the air and yipping. "Someone get a doctor!" She turned and pointed at the nearest ineffectual knight gaping at her.

"What would you have me do, my lady?" He was blond with a red tunic and steel braces on the front of his calves.

"Get a medic or a physician!" she shouted at him, feeling rage flooding in to replace the fear.

"We have nonesuch, my lady," a voice said behind her. She spun to see Kei looking stricken and grave, kneeling beside March and wiping his face with a square of damp cloth.

"Whoever it is that keeps your king alive with all his insides falling out, get him." Neva had always been very good in a crisis.

"He lives only through enchantment, and the how of that is not known to me. Would you have me bind your lord in the same way he has been?" Kei's voice held a lot of pain, and Neva hated him on reflex for March.

Neva didn't bother to protest the lord thing, because, for one, she thought he might mean Lord with a capital 'L' and she didn't want to examine that too closely. She didn't want to think about it at all. She definitely didn't want to get March all hooked up in another curse thing, but what if it was the only way to save him? He said he wanted to live. So being cursed was probably better than dead.

"You know how to treat battle wounds, though, right? You can staunch the blood at least and feed him whatever you feed people to get their blood up." She knew that didn't all make the most sense. But Kei seemed to get the message, because he nodded.

"Yes, my lady, that we can do." He waved and several men scattered, breaking into flat-out running as the crowd dispersed to let them through.

"Do you have someone who can track boar that I can use?" Neva watched March struggle to smile up at her, and she felt her heartbeat in her mouth. She was not going to let him die.

"May I ask why, my lady?" Kei stood up, and Neva realized he was young. His face was hard and tense like a soldier who couldn't afford to allow the possibility of humor, but he couldn't have been older than twenty-five. She sighed, knowing he was really ancient, and trying not to feel sympathy for him.

"I have to find Twrch Trwyth." That was all she told him. She could tell March trusted him not to murder him, probably having to do with some old-fashioned moral code, or—worse—maybe because once they had been friends, but she wasn't going to tell Kei that the boar was her only hope to save March. That seemed like something precious and secret.

The key felt hot and heavy in her palm.

"You only have to call him, my lady, and the boar will

come." Kei's voice fell like broken promises and torment between them, all sighs and long pauses.

Neva looked down at March, who winked, probably because smiling was becoming too difficult through the pain. She turned away, adjusting her hair, reaching down for Cafal, and strode towards the edge of the woods.

CHAPTER TEN

NEVA WALKED INTO the woods in what she hoped was a purposeful manner, stomping and kicking up leaves. Cafal followed behind, barking at her, excited. They wove through the trees, Neva trying to figure out exactly how she was supposed to find a pig who could think. Cafal trotted along behind her.

She felt the edge of panic under the calm façade of her purpose. March had seemed resigned, and that was never good. Resignation tended to produce the exact event a person was resigned over, Neva had always believed. It was a self-perpetuating cycle and when the end of that cycle was death, that was bad.

She heard voices close by and headed in that direction, even though she doubted it was the boar—but who knew in this place? In the way that this quest seemed to work, it could be some helpful person tossed into her path. A low rumbling started far away, a familiar noise she couldn't put a name to. Cafal barked louder. Neva continued through the trees, the voices getting louder.

She stepped out of the woods just as a plane flew overhead. Neva stood rigid, her heart beating in her throat. She was back home.

"Neva Jones! We've been looking for you all afternoon, girl. Where have you been?" Her granddaddy stood next to her car with his hat in his hand. One of her cousins was with him. They both blinked at her. "I didn't know you got a dog."

Cafal ran right over to him and jumped up against his leg. Her granddaddy smiled and scratched him behind the ears. Her cousin Jimmy watched her with a guarded expression.

"Nadia says you haven't been feelin' too good lately, Neva." Jimmy raised an eyebrow.

"Screw Nadia." Neva couldn't really process what was going on. Her heart felt like it had a dart run through it.

"Yeah, I always thought she was full of shit myself." Jimmy laughed and pulled his hat off to brush a hand through his hair.

Neva just stared at her car and her granddaddy's truck on the other side of it. The sun reflected off the metal, bright and looking hot to the touch. She could hear, far in the distance, the hum of traffic and the buzz of outboard motors.

"How about if I drive you home and Jimmy follows in my truck? You look like you're not feelin' too well." Her granddaddy approached her and wrapped his arm around her back. "Maybe got a heat stroke or comin' down with the flu. One time I had the flu so bad I thought I saw Stonewall Jackson in my yard. My hand up to God it's the truth."

He steered her over to the passenger side of car and

opened it for her. She got in automatically, folding herself down and reaching for the seat belt and staring straight ahead. She heard him open the back door and heard the sounds of Cafal leaping into the car. He rested his head on her shoulder from the backseat. When she reached up to him, he licked her fingers.

More than being jarred and puzzled, she was scared. If the dog was still here, if her granddaddy and cousin could see the dog, then he was real. If he was real, then March was lying on the grass somewhere a thousand years ago bleeding to death. There was no one who loved him to save him, to hold his hand as he passed on—as he died horribly—to just witness it.

Her granddaddy opened the driver's side door and reached down to let the seat back before he got in. He tuned the radio to a country station when he started the car and didn't try to make conversation on the drive back to her house. He rested a heavy hand on her forearm in silent comfort and then replaced it on the steering wheel. What he thought was going on didn't really matter to Neva. He wouldn't say anything to anyone about finding her wandering inexplicably around on his property or about her fugue state.

The main thing she couldn't quite process, that kept making itself heard in an echo to any other thought she had, was that if she was back home that meant she was released from the *geas* without completing the tasks. If she was released, March was dead. She'd seen him dying—he knew he was dying—and now she was back. There was no other conclusion to draw.

They pulled into the driveway, Willie Nelson on the radio singing about cowboys, and Jimmy pulled in right behind them. Jimmy left the engine running as they climbed out of her car and she let Cafal out to bound down beside her, his eyes staring up into hers with his head cocked.

Her granddaddy hugged her, his salty, working man's scent making the reality of the situation all the more final, breaking her in such a way that she needed them to leave so she could be alone with her grief and disconnection.

"If you need anything, call me." Her granddaddy patted her on the back, pressed her keys into her hand, and strode over to the truck. A car passed on the street. A cloud moved in overhead, throwing her yard into shadow. She turned toward the house, her whole body feeling heavy and uncooperative, and walked to the back door to let herself into the kitchen.

The cats didn't pay the dog any mind, which was a little strange—even in Neva's state she noticed that. She stood right inside the door of her kitchen, picturing March lying on his back in the grass with blood at the corner of his mouth winking to her. She thought about it for a long time, long enough that when she realized she had to pee it was getting dark outside. Or it was fixing to rain real hard, she couldn't tell.

She didn't leave the bathroom that evening. She climbed in the bathtub in her clothes and sat there, without even running the water, wondering why, if she was going to go crazy, it couldn't have been the good kind of happy-go-lucky crazy. She fell asleep at some point and woke feeling cold, with her back aching.

She climbed out of the tub and wandered into her bedroom to lay face first on her bed. She didn't cry. She was too numb.

The next day she woke up to find Cafal peering at her from the side of her bed with his tail in the air, making a slight whine. She remembered she hadn't fed him or given him any water. She hadn't ever fed him.

"Do you eat?" Her voice cracked around the words. Cafal twisted his head back and forth. He didn't talk, and that was disappointing. "Okay."

She climbed out of bed with her joints aching. Her blood sugar was low, she realized, when standing made her lightheaded. The air smelled like rain ozone from lightning, thick with humidity.

She fed Cafal cat food. There were still chicken and dumplings in the refrigerator, and she heated some up for breakfast. The sky was still dark outside, like the rain was pausing long enough to trick people into going outside to get caught by it again. She sat at her kitchen table feeling hollow for a long while.

The next couple of days passed like that—sleep, eat, shower, sleep. The dog stayed by her side and the cats climbed all over her, sensing in that way cats have for knowing when a person's sad or sick.

Tony stopped by to rummage through the fridge and hollered at her from the kitchen. "Baby girl, where y'all at?"

"Livin' room," Neva replied from her perch on the couch.

Tony microwaved something, singing Madonna to himself. Neva didn't really think she was prepared for company. She didn't know what to say to Tony. Cafal she could explain with an impulse trip to the pound—but her complete nervous breakdown? Not so much.

He strolled into the living room, swaying his hips, eating cheese grits out of a bowl.

"Good lord, what happened to you?" The spoon fell in the bowl and Tony made a comically shocked face. "You look like someone stole your pep and replaced it with depression-ade."

"Something like that." Neva scooted over to make room for him, pulling the afghan around her lap and knocking the crumpled box-worth of Kleenexes onto the floor.

"You did not just do that." Tony lifted an eyebrow and sat down.

"I did." This was going to be a trial, and she was too raw for it, too lost and scared and madly in love with either a figment of her imagination or a dead god. Either option was pretty much unexplainable and equally as bad.

"Lay it on me, who killed your cat?" He ate a spoonful of grits and talked to her with his mouth full—that's how she knew she must look like complete crap. Tony forgetting his manners? Not likely. "And did I mention you appear to have a dog?"

"His name's Cafal." She collapsed over the arm of the couch somewhat dramatically in an accidental way.

"Didn't know you were into the Arthurian legends, get out!" He made a little shriek in happiness. If she had been in her right mind, she would have kept that to herself. *Stupid, Neva,* she told herself. He was the most well-read person she'd ever met—he was a literature professor. Of course Tony would know about *all* of this, not just where Cafal's name came from.

"I'm not." He voice sounded weak in her own ears, and she felt that prickle of something being off. "What do you mean?"

"Caval, Cafal, girl, that's King Arthur's dog's name." He sat on the couch next to her as she gaped at him. "Your brain fall out your head?"

"Huh. He came with that name. He's adopted. King Arthur's dog? Hit me, what's the story? I don't remember King Arthur having a *dog*." Neva could see clearly in her mind the picture of the knights in the glade, hear the clanking of armor, hear March talking about original stories and betrayal. The King Arthur legend was all about betrayal, right?

"Well, that's probably because you only saw *The Sword in the Stone* or read *The Once and Future King.*" Tony paused to eat another bite of grits. "In the older stories, in the Welsh stories that the King Arthur legend grew out of, Arthur, or the characters that would eventually become Arthur, they had all kinds of named animals. Tons and bucket loads."

The hair on Neva's arms stood up. "Welsh?"

Tony lifted an eyebrow. "You science people are so ig'nant. Yes, Welsh. The real stories, the first, original stories were Welsh. Most of them can be found in the *Mabinogion,* this epic poem about cattle raids and epic quests after hair, wack stuff."

Neva blinked at him as her mind clicked and whirled. Her stomach pitched and thought about escaping through her mouth. "Mabonogon?" She approximated what Tony had just said. "What does the name mean?"

"Mabinogion. I don't really know, baby girl, this is totally outside of my field, but probably the Celtic god Mabon. He was a god of youth like Apollo, eternal youth and all that. He even made it into the actual Arthurian legends, I think. Something having to do with a pig hunt."

Neva almost broke into tears. This couldn't all be *real.* Not this real. Mabon was what Dahut and Magog and Mac had called March. March was the god of eternal youth? No freaking way. She felt like the insane-o-meter had just hit eleven.

"Have you ever heard of someone named something Mac Lir?"

"Sure, Manannan. The son of the sea, Irish sea god or something." Tony eyed her over his bowl of grits. "You run into some crazy pagans lately or something?"

Neva sort of half smiled at that before the expression collapsed into the slack expression she'd worn since coming back from the pond.

"Oh, I see what's goin' on here then." Tony set his bowl of grits on the table and grabbed Neva, pulling her halfway across his lap so that she was laying down and he was petting her hair. "Some man's doin' you wrong? You meet someone and been keeping it to yourself? A pagan someone, maybe? Into Dungeons and Dragons or some-such?"

Neva didn't say anything. The tears were right there, ready, and she didn't know what to say.

"Oh, I see. You're gonna be like that, huh? What's his name? And let me just say that any man not interested in you would have to be interested in *me* instead, because anyone not interested in you would have to be gay." He stroked her hair. His smell—smoke and citrus—was familiar, and she relaxed into him and let the tears flow.

"He's unavailable is all." She figured that was probably the best way around the truth.

"Oh, no, honey, you're too good for all that married man business." He sighed.

"Not like that, it's just complicated. He's got issues." Being dead was a serious issue and so was being imaginary.

"Crazy, huh? You always did like the difficult ones." He laughed at her.

"I guess that's about right."

"Tell me all about this crazy mofo, he up in the state mental hospital or what?"

"No, nothing like that." Nothing that good. "He's just difficult." Which was true, difficult and unreasonable and unreadable and complex.

"And fine, right? What's he look like? We do shallow around here." He jostled her and little and she could feel him start to braid her hair.

"He's tall, taller than you, even. His hair's black and wavy. Bluish-green eyes." She could see his face, his head thrown back laughing, his full red mouth open with his eyelashes brushing against his cheek, and she felt like she was dying a little bit.

"Oh yeah? Your type, huh?" He laughed. "I'm shocked, *shocked*! And he's probably got a bad attitude and a mean streak. He don't hit dogs?"

"Maybe a bad attitude. No hitting." Maybe he did, but Neva would give just about anything to have March sitting in the room trying to glare her into submission than what she actually had, which was nothing.

"Neva, girl, there'll be someone better." He tugged her hair a little. She knew he was totally wrong. There had never been anyone better, never in all of history, and he was gone.

Eventually work started calling to find out what she was doing, why she wasn't answering her email. She ignored the calls.

Her mom stopped by one afternoon. Neva got out of the shower and found her standing in the kitchen wiping the counter down with a rag. Luckily, she had showed up when Neva was clean and looking close to normal.

Her mom raised an eyebrow. "You haven't called me. You don't have any time for your mother?" She wiped in a disapproving way, frowning and flicking her wrist out in abrupt jabs at the counter top.

"I've been busy." Neva didn't have to fake the annoyance, which was her normal tone of voice when her mother tried to butt into her life unasked, which was a good thing all things considered. A very good thing. All she needed at the moment was her mom asking questions and being interested. When her mom got interested in something, Neva couldn't keep a secret away from her.

How she'd figure out that Neva had had a psychotic break and brought a dog home as a souvenir Neva didn't know, but she would.

"Too busy for your mother?" She lifted the other eyebrow and stuck hand on her hip. "You look like you got put through the wringer. Go put some clothes on, we're goin' to lunch at Wetzel's."

Neva didn't have the strength to argue. She got dressed, her mother hollering a running commentary from the kitchen as she did.

"Where'd that dog come from?" she asked when Neva returned to the kitchen dressed, her hair pulled back in a knot.

"He was a stray." Cafal looked at her from the corner where he was bedded down on the pillows she'd put there for him.

"Someone's real unhappy about that. That dog's some kinda huntin' dog. Probably cost a leg." Luckily her mom seemed to be letting that one pass under her radar. If her mother only knew Cafal's potential pedigree.

"Yeah, he's special." Neva smiled when he wagged his tail at her. Neva noticed her mom was wearing tiny apple earrings. She watched them swing as they drove to the restaurant. A weird dissonance settled on her as they pulled into the parking lot.

Lunch was normal. Normal was something Neva hadn't been looking to find. They ate oysters and drank a couple beers, and her mom filled her in on her gardening club. It was all prosaic and regular.

That was the first real step Neva made back to her life, to getting on with it and not just lying down and giving up. She dreamed about March, dreamed he was in the room with her, but in the daylight she had to maintain the masquerade that her life hadn't been completely blown apart in a way that left her no resources to figure out how to sort through the pieces.

One morning she got a crazy itch to go to the beach. It wasn't the season, and in the middle of winter it would be crawling with tourists from Indiana and Michigan, but she woke up and instantly knew she had to go. She got dressed in loose-fitting cotton pants and a long-sleeved t-shirt, grabbed her coffee to go, and loaded the dog into the car.

The sun was out, humidity sticking close to the ground. Even though it was February, it was sixty-something degrees outside and would get above seventy that day, for sure. Perfect weather, really. There were only a few weeks of it in south Alabama, and Neva took advantage of it. She drove out to the beach with the windows down, the smell of the sea getting stronger as she got closer, and she felt something close to contentment for a few minutes.

She wondered if March had liked the beach, what he would have looked like with a tan. Her half-smile collapsed when she pictured it clearly in her mind. The only thing that would have made the day better would have been him sitting in the passenger seat, complaining about having to get up so early just to go lay around somewhere else. She wondered if he had known how to drive.

Gulf Shores was full of Mardi Gras tourists. She parked across from the Florabama, in the parking lot the locals used, and crossed the busy highway more timidly than the dog. The beach clung to the coast in a narrow band south of Highway 182, changing names from Perdido to Orange Beach to Gulf Shores, a long stretch of pure white sand dunes and rapid growth. The condos blocked the sight of the beach from the highway.

Neva took off her flip-flops when her feet hit the sand,

letting them dangle from her fingers by the thongs, and she smiled at the familiar feel of the sand between her toes. Cafal ran ahead of her a little, then back again, over and over in enthusiasm. There weren't many people out yet. She walked down to the waterline and rolled her pants up above her knees. The beach curved out into the ocean toward the Florida line, and she walked along it toward Perdido Key, looking for shells and crying silently. Her heart was broken over someone who might not have even been real, or who, if he had been, was dead. Either way, she was bereft. She was alone with her memories, alone with her grief. Not even counseling held any sort of promise because a therapist would probably commit her. Something vital and fundamental was missing from her, and nothing she could do would change that. Ever.

"Look at this totally awesome one I found," a man said from behind her, and Neva was so startled she dropped all the shells out of her shirt back into the tide.

Manannan Mac Llyr, Mac, stood right there, water lapping around his ankles, his black hair darker still from water, with his hand out to her holding a perfect lace murex in his palm. The shell shone white, spines protruding from the tight spiral of its body. It was the sort of shell that people bought in tourist shops, they didn't just find them laying in the sand; the fragility of the thin, two-inch long spines and delicate curling lip of the mouth of the shell meant they weren't ever found intact by beachcombers.

She stared at him. He was just as handsome as before, bordering on beautiful. His expensive-looking sunglasses kept her from reading anything in his eyes. He wore a coral necklace, white against his deep tan. She couldn't see a single freckle on his skin.

"Like, if you're thinking this is a hallucination or

something, it's not." He tossed the shell in an arc into the breakers. "Check this out."

He turned so that his back was to a middle-aged couple sitting on a blanket up on the beach and dropped the back of his swimming suit, mooning them. "HEY!" The man shouted back at him. The woman just laughed and made a cat-call.

"What in the hell is going on?" Neva glared into Mac's smirking face. *This* was a god? She flipped through all her knowledge of Greek and Roman mythology and wondered if all those stories were *true*. Seduction and childish peevishness and randomness. Because this guy was the biggest frat boy who ever lived.

"Maybe I'm making my move." He said "moooooove" with the vowel stretched out, in a lascivious way, and he cocked his hip to the side, obviously making a joke.

"Maybe I'm gonna smack you in the side of the head." Her heart sped up and her stomach dropped out.

The constriction in her chest felt like hope. Hope that maybe this was a sign, that maybe March had survived somehow.

"That's harsh, dude, because I'm totally here to hook you up." He brushed his hair away from his face and smiled down at her.

"I know who you are." The words fell out of her mouth with a sort of finality that Neva knew was a key to something. That by admitting it to herself and to him, she was doing something almost magical, acknowledging what people no longer did, deeper truths. Now she was bound in a way she hadn't been before.

Mac's face cleared of the smirk for a second. "I know." Just as quickly, he went back to dimples and smarmy.

"How are you here to hook me up?" She couldn't bring herself to say more.

"Being the totally awesome guy I am, I brought you a present. I thought about putting the full-on whammy on you and making you my concubine or something, but that gets boring after a couple hundred years." He yawned in mock-boredom.

"Could you cut the shit and tell me what's going on?" Neva felt like she was on the edge of having a heart attack.

Mac twisted his head to the side and reached two fingers out to touch her face. "Except you might be worth the let-down when everything starts to suck."

She felt the world spin for a second, the tide turning into a whirlpool around her feet.

"I could give you every pearl in the ocean and a throne of coral. The mermaids would sing your name and the great beasts of the sea would honor you." The sun somehow maneuvered itself to halo Mac's head and he seemed to be hovering with just his toes in the water.

Neva stared at him in his glory. It might have been impressive if she wasn't in the middle of grieving and hoping against hope that Mac was here for something more important than just hitting on her again. "Is March alive?"

The scene shifted back to just Neva and Mac standing in the fingers of the tide, Cafal sitting above the waterline looking on. "Whatever, you belong to him. I give up. Can't blame a guy for trying." He shook his head and made a snorting noise. "No harm no foul."

"What is freaking going on here?" Neva shouted in his face, moving right up to his chest, so close she could smell the brine and seaweed on his skin.

"Don't be like that, dude. Did I mention that Mabon is sitting in your kitchen probably bitching to your cats about you not being home for his grand entrance?" Mac tossed his head back, laughing full-throated.

"What?" Neva stepped away from him and pulled her flip-flops out of the pocket of her pants and ran from the waterline up the beach.

"Don't look at me like that, I could totally smite you down or something. I had to get one more lick in, dude, so I called you out here to see if I had a chance. Don't get in my face about it." She stopped and looked over her shoulder at him. He looked slightly put out that she would be angry with him. A lock of dark brown hair materialized in the air. It was knotted up to keep all the hairs bound together.

"Is that . . . ?" She asked in rushed whisper.

The hair knotted itself and fell into the tide, disappearing almost immediately.

"I release you, Neva Jones." Mac sighed.

"Over and out, Neva," Mac said behind her as she ran towards her car.

The drive home was maddening. The traffic was completely out of control because of Mardi Gras, cars bumper to bumper on the one rural route that led from the shore to the interstate. Neva felt sick to her stomach. Adrenaline hit her blood and her mouth went dry. She wasn't sure if she was more worried that March would actually be in her kitchen or terrified that he wouldn't be.

She tore into her driveway, throwing rocks from under the tires and Cafal bumping against the dashboard. "Sorry," she told him, reaching over to open the passenger door to let him out.

The actual walk to the back door she took slowly, adrenaline having flooded her blood to saturation level. Everything around her seemed too bright, too sharp. The handle of the door felt hot as she twisted it. Inside, the kitchen was empty. She stood in the doorway, in the liminal space between desolation and resignation. Cafal threaded through the space between her leg and the jamb.

He trotted to the door to the hallway and stopped. His hackles rose and he growled in the back of his throat. Neva watched him, not really processing anything.

"I hate dogs," a voice groused from the hallway. "Stupid animals."

Neva stepped into the kitchen and left the door wide open behind her. She ran to stand behind Cafal to find March staring the dog down with his arms crossed over his chest.

"That thing's going to the pound." March lifted an eyebrow at her and lifted his chin before breaking out into the smile that stretched so wide it looked like it hurt. Her heart broke all over again just to see him. He was dressed in jeans and a ratty t-shirt with a snake twisting on the fabric right over his heart. He looked six kinds of perfect to her. He was eternal and apparently immortal, but that didn't matter, had never mattered. He was him, and that's all Neva cared about. March, not Mabon, an imperfect man with an attitude problem and the most perfect laugh in the universe. She stepped around the dog and lifted her arms up to him, and March picked her up and squeezed her so hard it hurt.

He pressed his face into the side of her neck, and his skin felt hot, just like it looked like it would with the perpetual blush on his cheeks.

"I thought you were dead." She twisted her fingers into his slippery soft hair. He laughed, the vibrations echoing from his chest to hers.

"I was." He spun them so her back was pressed to the wall and slid his mouth across her cheek to her mouth. He kissed away her silent questions and she breathed air straight from his lungs. He still smelled like the fresh air of the woods, of evergreen and a sharp tang like apple juice.

He pulled back from her, the hard muscles in his arms shifting, and frowned.

"What?" Her laugh spilled out at his hard expression. His anger amused her, which might not be the best start for a calm co-existence.

"You taste like the ocean." He set her down and stepped back to look at her sandy clothes.

"I was at the beach. Mac summoned me there on some adolescent prank." March's frown dissolved into a total glower. "What?"

"Typical. *And?* He summoned you and then what? He bound you with some kind of hex and now you have to live with him half the year in a palace under the sea?" March rolled his eyes and ran a hand through his hair.

"What? Have you lost your mind? What in the hell are you talking about? He summoned me there to steal your thunder. Hex me? Why would he hex me?" Neva rested her hand on his arm and he flipped it around so he could hold her hand.

"Because he was the one who set this up. He set the pieces in motion for me to be released from the *geas* by dying. He sped up the process after we ran into him." March sighed. "I just can't believe he did it with no strings attached."

"I thought you had to find your true love to be released from your curse." Neva couldn't really believe she said that, but she was under a lot of stress, and true love was hardly much of a stretch of the imagination when confronted with *gods*. March smiled and laughed in a bright, short spike.

"Yeah, I did, but there are always catches and loopholes. I had to end the cycle. That meant dying." He reached behind her head and unknotted her hair, running his fingers through it. "Died to that cycle and was reborn to a new one. A fresh start."

He was *really* her fairytale prince, her true love. Neva pressed her hand against the snake on his shirt and felt the solid muscle of his chest and thought, *This is real*. She stood on her toes as he ducked down to kiss her, mouth open and an edge of frenzy to it.

"Why's this door standing open like this? *Neva!*" Her mother's voice shouted from the kitchen. March turned his face in that direction.

"Who the hell's that?" He glared.

"Get used to it. No one ever knocks around here." She pulled him by the hand into the kitchen, and claimed her own fresh start.